Finding My Elf

DAVID VALDES

HARPER TEEN

An Imprint of HarperCollinsPublishers

Library of Congress Control Number: 2023933499
ISBN 978-0-06-328888-1

Typography by Jessie Gang
23 24 25 26 27 LBC 5 4 3 2 1
First Edition

To Ashley, Stacey, Jen, Amy, LeeAnna, Kristin, and Johnny
for seeing me through

Two Days till Elfmas

No one can accuse my dad of being subtle. He loves Christmas the way most guys in the Pioneer Valley love the Patriots. Instead of team jerseys, he has a collection of ugly holiday sweaters that would be kind of impressive if it wasn't so embarrassing. (Seriously, the llama one lights up. I can't.) So I shouldn't be surprised that when I arrive home for my first, or maybe last, winter break from college, the house looks like, I don't know, Frosty Con. Snowmen *everywhere*.

I'm so not in the mood.

Don't get me wrong: I like Christmas well enough. Even though Halloween is my favorite holiday because of the costumes, I *love* all the twinkling lights, and you can't really overplay "All I Want for Christmas Is You." But it's been a long day on the bus from NYC, and before it was a long day, it was a long week in a long semester. Not that I'm ready to admit that to my dad.

I purposely chose a bus that would get me home to Lindell

while he was working. Yes, it's, like, almost two miles from the bus stop in front of the old town hall to our place, but dragging my bag for forty minutes was worth it for the chance to come home to an empty house. I need some time alone in the privacy of my room before Dad gets here and I become the grinch, the carol killer, the fly in the eggnog.

I have to tell him that I'm failing out of school.

Okay, that's not entirely true. I'm passing freshman English and bio, which is a total shock based on my high school science grades. But I'm failing where it matters: my theater classes. They matter not just because that's my major but because I'm on scholarship. Or *was*. By the time grades come in, that scholarship will be past tense, and probably my NYU future along with it.

It's a huge relief to open the door to my bedroom and see that my dad is still honoring my personal space. Not a snowman in sight.

I don't even unpack before throwing myself across my bed, which looks exactly as I left it. When I boxed up stuff for college, I kept almost everything in my room as it was. New York is the biggest city in the country—why lug stuff with me when I can find whatever I want there? Besides, I was going there to reinvent myself, to start a different life from Cam here in Lindell, so why not wait to let the new me figure out my room?

I thought City Cam might change his hair, his clothes, his vibe. City Cam's friends might get him hooked on some new fandom, make him a stan for something Lindell Cam had never even heard of. City Cam—

City Cam's life didn't look like that *at all*. And now I'm back in Lindell, same as I ever was.

It's embarrassing how good it feels to be in my room again. It's small—our house is a Cape, so my room is where the attic used to be; the walls slant in on both sides. Ryan Gosling and Emma Stone dance across one on an oversized *La La Land* poster. Another wall is a shrine to all the Broadway shows I've seen in my life; there are ten Playbills, starting with *Matilda* and ending with *Six*. (There's plenty of room for adding shows I appear in someday.) A pride flag, the good one with the trans colors and the BIPOC triangle, covers the space above my headboard.

My eye falls on the mirror, which is framed by two pictures: to the left is me as Harold Hill in the *Music Man* my freshman year. In the photo, I look happily shocked, and for good reason. My dad—who *loves* gift-giving—found Hugh Jackman's agent online and begged him for an autograph to give a fellow Harold Hill. Hugh's that kind of guy, so right after curtain, my dad handed me a note that read: "The only trouble we got right here is finding the next show. Cheers, H. J." It felt like he was passing me the baton.

On the right side of the mirror, I am a very goth-looking Hamlet. The photo is black and white, which ramps up the kohl around my eyes and the glow of the lanterns we used instead of stage lights. I look older, more intense, not a silly kid singing about trombones, but a serious actor. Which is who I had become. After a summer acting intensive at a local college following my sophomore year, I ditched the *Annie*-loving musical theater kid I had been and focused on drama. I finagled my way into a workshop at Shakespeare & Company and got a part in *12 Angry Jurors* at Mercerville Community College the summer after my junior year. By the time I convinced Ms. Kropp to stage a futuristic *Hamlet* at Lindell, my transformation was complete. I was so proud of that production photo, I submitted it with my application to NYU.

Looking at it now makes me want to cry.

I roll onto my side, but the view's no better there. I'm facing an empty photo frame that used to hold a picture of Leroy, my last (okay, only) boyfriend, and me at prom. Leroy looks exactly like Corbin Bleu from *High School Musical*, which my dad put on TV like a babysitter when I was little so he could make dinner in peace. Leroy has a smile that melted me every time it broke across his face. And when he held me in his arms, I felt like a character in a rom-com.

So what did I do? I broke up with him after graduation because I didn't want Lindell Cam to get in the way of City Cam's whole new life. Everybody tells you not to do long distance in college, right? Leroy said he understood, but he still wouldn't talk to me for weeks; he gave me the silent treatment right until he started dating the next boy, Shay, a sun-kissed blond lifeguard from his summer camp job. As far as I could tell, they had nothing in common, and I had a sneaking suspicion it was pure revenge romance—which was fine by me. I had my next life to look forward to.

I kept the frame so that when I came back from school, I could put a photo of City Cam's boyfriend in it. But City Cam didn't have a boyfriend. He barely had dates. There were some cute boys at parties and a near miss with a guy from bio, who was an enthusiastic texter but a terrible kisser. There was never a chance of him filling the frame, which sits there empty.

Ugh. My own room is mocking me.

There is only one thing to do. Under my bed, a 1960s carry-on bag hides behind a clothes storage bin. I push the bin away and pull out the tote, which I've always pictured as belonging to a flight attendant with big hair and a cute scarf. Inside are two things: Kat Bizarro and a bag of Reese's Peanut Butter Cups.

Kat Bizarro was a find at a flea market when I was maybe five or six. Imagine a black Siamese cat—something which, I was bummed to learn, does not exist in real life—made of thickly knitted yarn. Green glass eyes are the only features on its diamond-shaped head, which sits atop a skinny neck connected to a bowling-pin-shaped body. There are three red buttons down its chest, as if it is wearing a suit, which it is not. It's heavier than it looks—I think the filling is dried beans—so maybe it was a doorstop in its first life. But at six I saw only a cat that liked dress-up, clearly a kindred spirit. I slept with it every night until I left for college, but I left it behind because I couldn't imagine showing it to a roommate. And boy, have I missed it.

With Kat Bizarro liberated once more, I rummage in the bag of peanut butter cups. I'm not so good at stopping once

I get started, but I keep an emergency stash on hand at all times because Reese's is the food version of therapy. The bag is not small. It's still half-full from this summer. I purchased it moments after I left the Berkshire Twin Cinema, where I'd ended up sitting behind Leroy and his BF, and discovered I was less cool with my post-Leroyness than I thought. On an average day, a handful of these babies would be enough, but tonight I'm going to kill the bag.

Then I call Jazz, whose break from UMass Amherst started yesterday.

"Finally," she says by way of answer. "You know if you'd gone to school in state, we coulda hung out last night, right? Why you had to go all the way to New York . . ."

"It's not that far!" I protest, mostly out of habit. Jazz always thought it was foolish for me to go to New York when I could save a ton by staying here at one of the state colleges in Massachusetts. She used every tactic: guilt (reminding me that I have a single dad who pays the bills by working two jobs), fear (Lindell is farm country by Massachusetts standards, so I have zero city-living skills), and shame (calling me a snob for thinking I'm too good for Lindell). I was determined that when City Cam came home all shiny and new, she'd see I was right.

This is going to suck; my pride is already wounded enough. But here I go. "Actually, maybe you're right."

"Huh?" Jazz's voice switches from teasing to suspicious. She doesn't hear "you're right" that often from me.

"Maybe I'll come home . . . uh, *stay* home."

"What? WHY? And don't tell me it's 'cause you miss me." She knows me so well: that was going to be my exact joke. "CAM . . ."

"I . . . I suck." I don't mean to cry, but I do as I tell her the whole deal. How I'd gotten placed into ETW, the supercool contemporary theater program, just as I'd hoped, only to discover I don't know much about contemporary theater and that I am *not* cool by New York standards.

"Come on," she says. "You got Lindell High to do *Urinetown*!"

I groan. "That's just it. What passed for bold and edgy in drama club here counts as tired and old-school there. These kids are doing one-person shows about their sex lives and absurdist comedies I don't understand that make fun of things I've never heard of. This one kid, no joke, did a modern-dance interpretation of AOC giving a speech."

"That's theater?" Jazz sounds genuinely puzzled.

"Right? That's what I've spent my whole semester asking myself." I start pacing around my bed. "Do I even *know* what theater is? And my teachers seem to be asking the same thing."

"*Damn*, Cam!" This is her favorite expression of sympathy, and it feels good to hear it, even though I know I have to turn down the offer coming next. "How fast can you get to Buzz?"

Lindell has two coffee shops: the world's smallest Dunks—which, naturally, my dad loves because we come from two different planets—and Buzz, which has this kind of '90s alt vibe going on. The logo is a cup of coffee being held by a wired-looking skater drawn by Rena, the owner. If I'd lived in the '90s, I think I'd have been more NSYNC than Nirvana, but I like Buzz because it's the closest thing to a queer space in this town. All of us (like, ten people, maybe?) and our friends hang out there.

Everyone else hangs at Denny's in the strip mall where Lindell meets Mercerville, which has like ten thousand people and feels, comparatively, like a metropolis. Denny's booths fill up with hungry Lindell High kids about twenty minutes after last bell on weekdays. And whenever there's a basketball or hockey game, the place is packed, win or lose. Late-night study sessions, pre-prom pancake runs—Denny's is a core part of Lindell High life. Even though I put in my time working there, Denny's was never my spot. Being a Buzz regular instead has always been a point of pride to me; it tells you who I am and who I am not in this town.

"I can't go now," I tell Jazz. "My dad'll be home soon, so . . ."

"Ohhhh." If wincing makes a sound, that's what I'm hearing. "What're you gonna say?"

I throw myself back on my bed, holding Kat Bizarro to my chest like a shield. "Um, 'Hey, Dad, for Christmas, can I have a new life?'"

"Seriously."

Ugh. "I don't want to say *anything*."

"Then don't. I mean it," she says firmly. I sit up—that isn't what I expected, so I'm listening. "First, make Dad dinner." (Yes, she calls him Dad too, though she has one of her own.)

That's genius. When I was growing up, he did his best as a single parent, cooking every night after working all day. But I got pretty tired of homemade mac and cheese, chili, and taco night, which I know makes me a bad human because we had plenty to eat and all from scratch. But he loves habit like he loves tradition, so we pretty much ate the same six meals over and over—seven, if you count takeout from Lucky Sun, where our order never varies. I started teaching myself how to cook when I was in ninth grade, and it was a big win. Dad loved it, no matter how much I screwed up, and I could guarantee that there would be at least one meal a week that we hadn't eaten the week before.

I'm already on my way to the kitchen as Jazz goes on. "Let him have a good night—you don't have to lie, but only tell him the parts that don't suck for now. Like, tell him you met a cute boy or you climbed the Statue of Liberty or whatever. And then meet me at Buzz when it opens tomorrow. We'll figure out the rest there."

After reminding her that she is THE BEST, I start in on carbonara, Dad's favorite. I put water on to boil before going to the fridge for bacon, eggs, and cheese. When I swing the door open, I hesitate. The lone carton of eggs only has four left; I need three. If Dad plans any early baking for the Cookie Party next week, he's screwed. I forge ahead and snag all but the last even so.

I tell Siri to play All-Christmas Radio. The room fills with Brenda Lee, and soon I'm the one rockin' around, slicing bacon into little strips to sauté with wine, whisking garlic and Parmesan cheese into the eggs. Carbonara is, like, the easiest thing to make that still always seems impressive. I heat the water now so that as soon as Dad walks in, I can throw the pasta in the pot, and we'll only have ten minutes of awkward conversation before we're eating.

By the time the water is at a boil, I feel less blue. Kelly Clarkson is belting "Wrapped in Red," and I am too, metal spaghetti tongs for a microphone. I do a spin around the bar in the middle of the kitchen and sing for all I'm worth. I can't wait to meet a guy who will appreciate it when I serenade him. Leroy found my singing embarrassing, something to endure because he loved me. For now, my audience is limited to snowmen, listening with button eyes and goofy fake coal grins.

"Cam-Cam!"

My dad's voice startles me so much I whirl on him, brandishing the tongs like a weapon. My heart pounds. Lost in the song, I hadn't heard the door.

"Dad!" Surprising both of us, I give him a hug, a real one. Mostly these days he gets a quick squeeze and a grimace when he kisses me on the cheek. Tonight, between the song and the smell of bacon and the being home of it all, well, call it a momentary lapse in cool, but I hold on tight for a minute.

When I pull away, there are tears in his eyes. God, he's corny.

"I—I'm making carbonara," I stammer, even though this is perfectly obvious.

"My favorite!" he says on cue. If there is any chance of me getting through this night, sending him into a lipids coma with cheese and bacon is my best bet.

Dad being Dad, he dives in before I have even gotten the spaghetti into the boiling water. "Tell me!" he says, rubbing his hands together. "Tell me everything."

Thinking about Jazz's plan, I try to convince myself that it's not a crime to omit a few facts as long as everything I *do* include is true. (Honestly, that practice got me through high school.) So I tell him about Kai, the Orientation Leader who flirted with me, and then about the teacher who said my voice was soothing. I recount the time I made my audience cry with a monologue about how Otto, our schnauzer, died. My dad laps it up, not knowing that Kai didn't know who I was when I ran into him in the dining hall the next day, or that the teacher who said my voice was soothing was criticizing me for a lack of intensity. My dad'll never know that the "audience" for my monologue was my RA, who cries at every Pixar movie and sometimes even a good commercial. They would *so* get along.

Dad is totally enrapt: he's barely eating his pasta. He has no idea I'm putting on a show, and his happiness keeps me going. If nothing else, it's the best acting I've done all semester.

But when I finish the tears-for-Otto story, my dad doesn't follow up with a question. He just looks at me, eyes still brimming. Fear flashes through me. Oh god—is he sick? Did he lose his job?

"Dad?" I'm afraid to ask what's wrong, and yet I have to.

"Cameron . . ." *Oh no.* He never says my full name. Does he know I'm failing? How would he? "I'm just so . . ."

Disappointed. That's what he's going to say. I brace for it.

". . . *happy* for you." He's so choked up he can barely eke out, "You finally found your place. It's all been worth it. I can't wait to call your tías!"

Now he eats, digging into the pasta with gusto, but I've lost my appetite.

Because he doesn't know the truth: his son the actor is really his son the liar.

One Day till Elfmas

Looking at myself in the mirror, I sigh.

Senior year, I ditched the short side-part haircut I'd had forever to grow out a long two-block with a center part, a look I fell in love with when I got hooked on K-pop. It took forever to grow my coppery-brown hair long enough to cover my forehead, so there was an awkward hat-wearing period in the middle, and it seemed like at one point or another, the entire population of Lindell told me I needed a trim. In a town of buzz cuts, whiffs, and fades, I stood out.

Then I got to New York and I didn't anymore. I wasn't even the only guy in my program with my haircut. The *really* cool guys had punky mullets or Olly Alexander bowl cuts, both of which would look nightmarish on me. By the standards of NYU, I was kind of dull.

I'd never felt that way in Lindell. I'm not a flashy guy, but while my classmates were wearing sweats and hoodies, I was putting together fun looks from vintage stores. In my senior picture, I'm wearing a '70s-turtleneck-and-gold-chain combo, a look both retro *and* on point. (For one thing, gold always makes my green eyes pop.) Sitting in my biology class between Geena, with her endless supply of school-day pajamas, and Carhartt-addicted, steroid-inflated Alex "Flex" Fleckman, I sometimes felt like an alien beaming down to Planet Normcore.

At NYU, the roles were reversed. I was the normie next to my roommate and semi-nemesis, Sarah Xu, who rocks granny dresses with platform Doc Martens and does performance art in public spaces, occasionally getting arrested. She and her whole crowd seem to live at the intersection of arty and bonkers, and are privileged enough to overshoot both. I find them all intimidating because they just seem so sure of who they are.

The Cam in the mirror looks confident enough at first glance. I'm wearing an oversized chunky emerald-green sweater and a thick silver chain, a look I got from Jungkook in BTS. I know it's a good color on me, but even I can see doubt in my eyes. Does my outfit say "cool kid back from college" or "trying too hard"?

Doesn't matter. I'll be late if I don't leave now, and Jazz is too type A to put up with that behavior. Fortunately, Dad has left me the car, a red Honda Fit that's as old as I am. It's a kindness for him to give me the car; taking the bus doubles his commute time. I felt guilty enough already—but not so guilty that I don't take the Fit now.

★ ★ ★

Like most weekday mornings, Buzz is half-empty, just a few tables occupied by adults on laptops. There's Earbuds Guy, who is always grooving to music you can't hear while he works, and Bags, which is what Jazz nicknamed this woman who comes in first thing with a backpack, a purse, and a tote, then sets up camp for hours. Jazz has our favorite booth, which sits beneath an honest-to-god full-sized Harley, which is bolted to the wall but still kind of scares me.

She looks so beautiful. In a cream-colored sweater and plaid pants, she pretty much screams Ivy League college student, minus the actual Ivy League. Her hair is a shock: gone are the box braids she favors, swapped not for her usual holiday weave, but for hot-pink close-cropped curls. The cut accentuates her to-die-for cheekbones, which seriously could have made her a model if her parents hadn't pooh-poohed that path as frivolous. Looks like college is going better for her than for me, but then I remember: appearances are deceiving. Does it make me a bad person to hope that maybe she too has got some terrible story to tell?

Nope. Over chai lattes, I find out that, in fact, she *is* rocking Amherst. She has all As despite working, multiple weekly rehearsals for her campus bhangra dance club, and practically living with her Norwegian girlfriend, Annika. I'm happy for her, right, but it hurts a little: she's the Jazz we both imagined she would be back when we used to sit in this same booth talking about how we couldn't wait to escape Lindell.

We'd always agreed that our town was too small, too tradi-
tional, too much a rinse-and-repeat cycle of kids growing up just
like their parents. *We* were the kids who went to Northampton
to watch art-house movies and sucked up the two-hour drive
to Boston to hear the bands too cool to play in Springfield.
Gay and Cuban American, I was a diversity double-dipper
at Lindell; Black, Jewish, and queer, Jazz was a full-on triple.
No surprise that we led both the George Floyd walkout *and*
the Don't Say Gay solidarity march. *Of course* we ended up at
Amherst and NYU.

"So what went wrong?" she asks now, leaning forward with
her brown eyes searching mine.

What *did* go wrong? "Everything, maybe? We did all these
weird, super-emotional exercises, and everybody else took them
so *seriously*. We read really dark, confusing plays, and I pre-
tended I was into them, but I wasn't. And my classmates just
seemed to get it—no, not just get it, but *love* it. And I'm like,
what's my deficiency?"

I know I sound kind of pathetic, but she's not judging. "So
much for classes. Were you in any good shows?"

"It's like a cruel joke. First-years don't even get to act. We just
crew other people's productions, and like, they're all in these
weird, tiny spaces. I did lights for a spoof of Harry Potter with
J. K. Rowling as the villain instead of Voldemort—"

"Honestly, that sounds amazing."

"It would have been, but there wasn't a light grid. I literally
sat on a ladder manually moving the spot and changing gels for

different scenes. The show was three hours long, and my legs were so numb that I couldn't actually climb down without help, which was, you know, the zillionth humiliation of the semester at that point."

This is where your average friend would tell you that "it'll get better" or "just hang in there," but Jazz isn't average in any way. "Remind me again how much you're paying to be free labor?"

I sink into my seat. "Once my grades are in, I'll be paying ten thousand dollars more than I was."

"They can take your scholarship away? Damn, Cam!" She shakes her head. "There's really nothing you can do?"

I shrug. "I don't think so. It's based on maintaining a three-point-oh."

"When are you going to tell Dad?"

I stare at the foam on my chai like it's a tarot card reading. But I don't find any wisdom. "I guess when the grades show up and it's official."

"What about Mari and Ely?" she asks, knowing how I usually confide in my tías.

"God, no, that's worse. They're terrible liars—their faces give them away. My dad would totally find out."

She looks skeptical. "Can you really hide this from him that long?"

"I have to. You know the Cookie Party is Dad's favorite day of the year—and that's still nine days away. And then Christmas is two days after. I can't ruin either." I drum the tabletop with my fingers. "Maybe I can get a part-time holiday gig somewhere." I try to picture myself back working at Denny's, taking orders from old classmates. "It would keep me out of the house as much as possible, and I'm gonna need the money."

Jazz's eyes get wide. "*Vision!*" she shouts.

That's a pretty big word for my half-baked plan. "I know you want to see me in a Denny's shirt, but—"

"No, Cam, *Vision*. The Shops at Vision Landing!"

"Wait—it's open?" When I left for school, they were still putting finishing touches on a brand-new luxury mall on the far edge of town, which used to be acres and acres of farmland. I've only seen it from outside: a sprawling complex of white interlocking cubes of different heights that together look super sleek and honestly way more LA than cow country. The local press has been talking it up for years, hyping both the economic impact and what a long way Lindell has come, from pastures to Prada.

"You have to see it to believe it. They cut the ribbon on Black Friday, and the parking lot was full all day. It's supposed to hold a thousand cars! And the new exit they made off Route 2 was backed up six miles."

"It's that good?"

"It's that *new*." She laughs. She digs in her bag for her phone. "God knows we need new around here." She scrolls through her photos and holds one up. It shows an atrium rising to skylights, flanked with three colonnaded levels of better-than-Lindell stores. "It's almost self-consciously posh. They call the upper levels 'the galleries' and the food court 'the Commons.'" She puts the phone away. "More important, they hired, like, half the county for the holiday rush. You'll definitely find something."

"I don't know. . . ." Say "mall job" and the only "vision" that comes to mind is me being stuck in a Spencer's dealing with middle schoolers who think it's edgy.

"Think of it this way: Where better to meet a cute boy for a little fa-la-la? You look like you need it." I'm contemplating this—she's not wrong—when she claps her hands as if to say *problem solved* and stands. Are we done?

"You wanna go right now?"

"As in go *with* you?" She gives me a look like I'm addled. "You don't need me to hold your hand. You're a big boy." She looks at her phone. "And Annika is probably awake now, so . . ."

"She's at your place?" I can't help it: I feel jealous, picturing Annika hanging out with Jazz's family.

Jazz doesn't seem to notice. "It was too expensive for her to go all the way back to Norway, and my parents love her, so . . . It's our first Christmas together."

Oh my god: Jazz is living my dream. I try to look happy for her but I fail, and she purses her lips. "This is where you'd say, 'Cool, when do I meet her?' Unless you need to get over yourself first."

She's right. I try to sound enthusiastic. "Cool—when do I meet her?"

"*After* you get a job." She hugs me. Is it briefer than usual? "Text me and see what we're up to later."

★ ✳ ★

Human resources doesn't exactly roll out the welcome mat. The woman who helps me has no problem shaming me with a reminder that holiday hiring season was weeks ago. Nonetheless, she hands me a job application for Santaland, the only place with an opening, and a map for how to find it, as if I'd somehow missed an entire Christmas village on my way in.

Filling the entire rotunda of the biggest wing of the mall, Santaland looks inspired by Whoville. Lines of restless parents and kids snake through lanes flanked by whimsical snow-covered houses. The idea of wrangling sugared-up brats as they whine for a glimpse of Santa has zero appeal. As I join the queue, I'm debating whether this will be worse or better than Denny's.

I started busing tables at Denny's my junior year. Busing—er, being a "service assistant"—is thankless; aside from the paycheck, there is little upside. Unlike waitstaff, you don't get to interact with the good customers, but you do have to deal with the wreckage left by the bad ones. When it's kids who know you, it can be even worse: the ones who like you are sure you won't mind dealing with their mess; the ones who don't are happy to make your job as hard as possible.

Eventually I became a server, increasing my income but also landing me on the front line with classmates, which varied from okay to really depressing. It was no fun having people my age giving me orders or withholding my tip when their food took a long time to arrive, as if I had personally cooked it. I quit spring of senior year so I could dedicate myself to preparing for

Hamlet. It hurt my wallet, but I considered it an investment in my future.

Standing in the molasses-slow Santa line, I check out my future workspace. The elves I see are mostly directing traffic or making cheerful small talk to keep people occupied; half the job seems to be facilitating selfies. Some have elf ears but no hat; some have hats but no ears. And they're all ages, which surprises me a little; I never thought of elves going bald or sporting laugh lines, but there are a couple who look older than my dad. (Come to think of it, he would crush elfdom.)

A worker my age catches my eye. He has wild dark curls that fall over his elf ears and perfectly smooth white skin, so I instantly christen him Timothée Chalamelf. I watch him swiveling through various family groups with a dancer's grace as he keeps the line moving. He seems to feel my eyes on him, and he flashes me a smile brighter than the fake snow on the rooftops. Suddenly the mall delivers on the Vision thing: I can see us hanging up our elf costumes at the end of a shift and heading out of the mall together holding hands. . . .

"Do you have any kids with you?"

I turn to see a white elf with blond hair plaited into two long braids that hang from her jaunty cap to well below her shoulders. She eyes me with suspicion as I stammer, "Um, no?"

She crosses her arms and narrows her blue eyes. "This is a family area. No one gets to see Santa without at least one child under twelve."

"Santa's not what I'm here for." That came out a little creepy, so before she can reply, I add, "I'm here for Victor. I'm—I'm—supposed to be an elf."

Her lips part in an "ooooh," and her demeanor immediately brightens. "Then why are you in this line? You'll end up on Santa's lap, not in Victor's office."

She unhooks a velvet guide rope and pulls me through a doorway into one of the houses. A long empty corridor runs the length of the village between the cheery facades customers can see and the store interiors, which they cannot. The only decorations are signs proclaiming various Elf Rules. She introduces herself as Miranda while we pass posters admonishing "Don't be a vector: Wash your hands" and "Elves don't hit back!" before she ushers me through a Staff Only door into a big room.

Christmas music from the village wafts in over the speakers, but there is no one around to hear it but us. One wall is dominated by a tinsel-framed marquee that reads "Santaland Command Center." Another features four prefab changing-room stalls marked "Helpers & Elves," though I don't know what the difference is. With two cheap desks and a long plastic lunch table surrounded by folding chairs, this "command center" clearly doubles as office and break room. Honestly, it's a little depressing.

Miranda points to a door with a sign that says, "ELVES HAVE NO GENDER." "There's only one bathroom and usually a dozen of us on duty, so don't drink a lot before your shift, and if you're doing any elf makeup, maybe do it before you get here. Victor's very time-sensitive—once you clock in, he wants you in Santaland."

I'm trying to imagine what elf makeup looks like when Victor himself enters from a door across the room. With olive skin, heavy eyebrows, and a thick mustache that doesn't reach either side of his smile, he looks like a Portuguese Charlie Chaplin. He's all of five foot two inches, including the mop of curls atop his head, which bounce as he hurries over to meet me. He snaps his fingers for my completed application, which I hand over somewhat reluctantly.

"Auditions were weeks ago. You know that, right?"

Weeks ago, I wasn't expecting to work over Christmas at all. But I don't say that. I am stuck on the word "auditions." Part of me is excited: I'm really good at auditions. But part of me feels sick: if I fail my audition for an *elf*, I don't think I'll ever recover.

I answer his question about my lateness, aiming to work the sympathy angle, pulling what Jazz calls "the full Chihuahua": making my eyes so big and full of need it's hard to resist me. "My family has fallen on hard times recently, and I'm just trying to help out." ("Hard times"? What is this, a Dickens novel?)

Impervious to my Oliver Twist routine, he lists the requirements: shifts are twelve to eight, with a half-hour lunch and a floating fifteen-minute break. To be an elf, you must commit to every day, weekends included, through the twenty-sixth. No one can be *compelled* to work more than six days in a row—a fact he announces like it's a terrible governmental overreach—but an employee may choose to, so the seventh day pays double to sweeten the pot. "Whatever you do," he says, "do not take this job if you need a day off."

The hourly rate is higher than I ever got at Denny's, and the notion of one day paying like two is appealing, so I assure him I wouldn't dream of it. It'll be so much easier to hide from Dad this way, though I'll have to figure out how to work around Cookie Party. I swap out the full Chihuahua for my best golden retriever expression, eager to please. "Honestly, it sounds perfect!"

I guess I'm going to lie a lot this vacation.

"You act?" he asks curtly.

"Yes, I played Hamlet last year. Maybe you saw—"

"And sing?"

Why would he ask that? Behind him, Miranda motions for me just to go with it.

"Yes. Very well."

"How much babysitting have you done? Or summer camp—have you worked at a summer camp?"

"Um. I was lead counselor at Broadway Arts Academy." I'm praying that he doesn't know it was only a one-week day camp for middle schoolers.

Victor purses his lip. "CPR certified?"

"Yes." (Okay, six years ago in Scouts, but it's not like the process has changed.)

"And you can work every day we're open till Elfmas is over?"

Oof. Do I ask about Cookie Party now or hold off till he knows me better? I plaster on a smile. "Of course!"

Victor unclips his walkie-talkie and raises it. "Command to Marco. Command to Marco. SCC pronto." He listens but gets only white noise in reply. Maybe Marco is the cute boy I saw in line? If I could put *him* on my Christmas list, I would.

"Bring me the Good Elf Playbook," he barks at Miranda, sounding like a general marshaling soldiers. I stifle a laugh, but he can see it in my eyes.

"Yes, I take things seriously. The holiday entertainment sector is a key player in the launch of the Shops at Vision Landing. Customer engagement here in Q4 will translate to loyalty in Q1." He keeps going with all kinds of corporate jargon, but I'm not so much listening as looking like I am. More acting!

Miranda hands Victor a big black binder, which he riffles through speedily. He opens it to a page of dialogue. The headline reads, "Tired Mom Scenario #3." I'd bet a million dollars there's no Tired Dad scenario in the binder, because the whole world acts as if families like mine don't exist.

I scan the text and see that it's suggested lines to use in an encounter with a frazzled parent who complains that the visit with Santa is too short for the length of time they stood in line. Oh my god—is this what my vacation will really be like?

A *different* handsome elf—Marco, I'm guessing—bursts into the room with the energy of the lead husky on a dogsled; honestly, it's hard to take. He strides over, smiling so broadly that dimples become canyons in his tan face. An elf hat barely stays on atop thick jet-black hair long enough that he has it pulled back into a ponytail. "New elf in town! What!" And then, seriously, he fist-bumps me, fluttering his fingers as he pulls back his hand. "I'm John-Marco, but everyone calls me Marco!"

Oh my god. This kid is dialed up to a hundred—not just *vibrating* with positivity, but actually bouncing. He's going to be exhausting to work with. I try to catch Miranda's eye—I so need to share an eye roll with someone—but she is grinning, and when she glances at me, she shoots me a look that says, *Isn't he great?*

"Tired Mom #3," says Victor, without preamble. Marco doesn't even have to look. He immediately slumps his shoulders and adopts an aggrieved look.

"We waited in line for an hour." He sighs in character. "And you're telling me we get two minutes with Santa?"

I hurriedly glance at my scripted response. "We appreciate you being so patient. We know that's not easy with a little one." I cringe. "A little one"? Who talks like that? (Mall elves, I guess.)

"Do you know how disappointed Manny is going to be? Do you even care?" He drags out the word "care" in a voice that is the verbal equivalent of the full Chihuahua. He's not terrible.

Despite their being no "Manny" in sight, my next line is "Are you excited to meet Santa?" and I sell it. I have to admit, a little grudgingly, it's impressive how the script never answers the mom's questions, instead deflecting her with praise and steering Manny toward the right attitude.

"Yes!" chimes in Miranda, filling in the gap in the dialogue. Victor looks pretty happy with me so far, and Marco, well, of course he looks happy. He's like a puppy; if he had a tail, it would be wagging.

With saccharine cheer, I deliver my closer. "A happy memory is just around the corner. Those two minutes will last Manny's whole life! Thank you for visiting Santa's Village."

"NO!" The single syllabus fires like a bullet, and Victor's face is mottled red. "If Mom wants to call it Santa's Village or the North Pole, or even *Hell*, let her. But ELVES say *Santa-land*." Without looking back over his shoulder, he points at the marquee. "This is a business. Branding matters."

Marco and Miranda exchange worried glances.

I've blown it. Fifteen minutes ago, I didn't even want this job. Now I'm crushed that I can't have it.

Victor hands the binder back to Miranda, while looking me up and down. "Get him a medium. It might be a little tight, but I'm not having sloppy elves." And with that, he pivots on his heels and leaves. I'm hired after all.

Marco raises a hand for a high five (who does that?), and I play along to not be an asshole. Miranda hugs me, despite having met me, like, twenty minutes ago. "I'll get you a helper suit for now so you can shadow Marco for a shift," she chirps, leaving me alone with the jolliest elf ever. Ugh.

He's intent on making me feel better about Victor. "He's not a bad guy, just really intense. The mall is depending on

Santaland to bring in serious revenue, so I think he feels a lot of pressure. I know I wouldn't want his job."

Oh good: cheery *and* earnest. Denny's is beginning to appeal to me. . . .

Okay, so this is NOT the job for me. Beyond the fact that I am never getting used to jingling with every step I take, I can't deal with these kids. They all want something: Can they touch my hat? Can I take a picture of them? Can I tell them a story? (Yes, a tragic tale of the boy who failed out of theater school.) And the questions!

From the parents:

- Do I know how much longer till they get to Santa?
- Is there a bathroom inside Santaland?
- Can I whisper x, y, z to Santa so he doesn't screw up Christmas morning?

From the kids:

- Do I sleep at the North Pole at night?
- How did I get the job with Santa?
- Why don't I have pointy ears?

It's exhausting. But not for Marco. Mr. Perky here is unflappable. He doesn't miss a beat when a little girl, her face turning Grinch green, yaks into a snowbank as if expelling a demon.

Marco reveals a working exit hidden in plain sight as the door to a Ye Olde Candle Shoppe. He ushers me, the girl (her color improving by the minute), and her exhausted-looking grandmother into the staff corridor, bringing us to a Comfort Room with a first aid cabinet, a fridge stocked with water and ginger ale, and two sofas—all done up Santaland style.

When he rings a bell, Mrs. Claus enters. With a voluminous white granny wig only slightly paler than her skin and glasses perched on the end of a button nose, she looks right out of central casting. "What a good girl," she croons. "Santa can't wait to meet you!" She doesn't even look our way but waves a chubby hand at us, signaling that we are not needed.

Once I have Marco alone in the hallway, I ask him how often that happens.

He shrugs. "Every day is different! I once had a kid with a nosebleed who tried to stop it by sticking a candy cane up his nostril. Wild, right?" He flashes the whitest of smiles, so bright I'm a little self-conscious. "That's why it's so fun to work here. You never know what's next. You'll see."

No, my bouncy friend, I won't. There is no chance I'm staying.

"I'd keep this gig even without the five thousand dollars."

I don't have elf ears, but my own work just fine.

Five thousand dollars?

Back in the command center, Marco hands me a tablet open to a page titled "12 DAYS OF ELFMAS!" God, the cringe never ends at this place. "How could you not know? Everybody's talking about it!"

Everybody in Lindell, maybe. There's no point saying the

news hadn't exactly reached New York City, so I bite. "What exactly is Elfmas?"

"It's a play on the word Christmas, but with—"

"'Elf,' I get it!" There's a two-second flicker in Marco's eyes, probably contemplating whether I am elf material. "Sorry, I just—what does it *mean*?"

"It's Victor's idea. A kind of *Big Brother* or *American Idol* for elves. Five challenges over the next ten days and Top Elf announced the day after Christmas—which is the twelfth day of Elfmas."

I'm intrigued. I almost don't want to know what an elf challenge is (though I bet it's mortifying), but it scratches my reality-TV itch. I have so many old seasons of *Survivor* downloaded on my computer that I barely have room left for anything else. From *Amazing Race* to *Drag Race*, competition is like candy to me.

I'm hooked now. "Okay . . . so what are the challenges?"

Marco shakes his head. "Nobody knows but Victor and Fiona. He doesn't want us to have an advantage."

"Who's Fiona?"

"The assistant manager—she plays Mrs. Claus."

"She looks all right," I say, proving I can be sort of positive too.

Marco works hard to reply. I can see his sweet side wrestling with something else that he wants to say. Of course, nice wins. "That means she's doing a good job!"

I'm sure there's a story, but I'm not here for gossip. I want to know about the cash.

"Is the five thousand dollars all for one elf, or do we split it?"

"Just one. We all get a little bonus for completing the challenges, but the real money is for the last elf standing."

An African American man way too old for his elf costume comes in, clearly on a mission. "Marco, Victor wants you back in the lanes. There's a slowdown by the Reindeer Corral."

Marco flashes that smile again. If he wasn't so irritatingly cheerful, it'd be cute. "Psyched that you've joined us, Cameron. Sorry we have to compete!"

He looks like he might hug me, but I forestall that with a wave. "Thanks for showing me around!"

When he's gone, the room feels a little grimmer, but at least I don't have to keep up with his chirpiness. The older elf, Larry, removes his cap, revealing a shiny dome. Soon, he's pulling off his slippers and rubbing feet in a state that I don't really need to see. The yellowing nails are like warnings to never grow old.

"That kid," he says. Ooh, maybe Grandpa Elf has dirt. I'm so down to hear the sordid truth about Perky.

Instead, he says, "How's anyone supposed to compete with that? He's like the factory-floor model of Christmas spirit! You got a better chance winning the lottery."

This is not the dirt I hoped for.

"You think it's a done deal, with all these elves?"

Larry shakes his head. "*All?* There's only five. Four before you showed up."

"But I saw more than that in line!"

Larry is rubbing the life into his feet, and I really, really wish he would stop.

"Oh, those are just helpers," he says. "Just" helpers? Has he *seen* Chalamelf? I wonder if there are any rules against, like, elf-helper liaisons.

Larry has no idea what I'm thinking, thank god. "Helpers steer traffic, clean up messes, that sort of thing," he says. "They don't even get elf names."

I guess this means helpers are Santa's service assistants. I try to put a positive spin on it. "Oh good, I'd hate being stuck on cleanup."

"Sorry, kid, but we do that too." I'm back to hating this job. "On a day-to-day basis, the biggest difference is that elves are the only ones allowed in with Santa. That and we don't have to wear the ears, which is how you tell us apart."

"So, no ears and a shot at five thousand dollars. You'd think people would be *all* over it."

He looks at me, puzzled. "Except that you have to work *every day*, which means either you have no life or you need extra cash to pay for the one you have." I want to protest, but he's still talking. "Mostly, though, I'd bet what keeps folks from applying is the pressure."

"Of competition?"

"Of being *watched*." Huh? "Everything we do will be on YouTube and Instagram. Victor wants a big social media following. He says more votes means more visitors—"

"Votes?"

"You thought Victor would pick the winner? Or what, a celebrity panel with Frosty, Rudolph, and Cindy Lou Who?" Okay, so I hadn't given it much thought.

The truth is dawning. "You mean—"

"It's a popular vote. The public decides. Hope you have a lot of friends." He heads for an elf changing room. "Tell everyone you know."

Who would that be? All the people I told I was too good for this town. The people to whom I made it clear that my future was in Times Square, not Lindell. The people I thought I'd left behind.

I think I've come up with my elf name: Screwed.

First Day of Elfmas

My dad is so excited for me about this job, it's like having an in-house Marco. Ever since I got home last night, he's been hounding me with elf names: Happy or Cookie or Hermey, after the misfit in *Rudolph the Red-Nosed Reindeer*. He even suggested Feliz, but I'll pass, since I've already endured a whole lifetime of Lindell people mispronouncing my last name, Ceballos. Seh-BUY-yos—it's not that hard, people.

Jazz suggested Sassy, but it felt a little on the nose. I decide to go with the name Kodi, after Kodi Smit-McPhee, who's my acting icon the way Hugh Jackman was my musical theater icon. Kodi the Elf rolls off the tongue easily, and the spelling is interesting. (I would so never be a mere Cody.)

It's not just me choosing. The elves who were hired before me have been going by their own names so far, but the launch of the competition means announcing our new Elf identities to the world. As I shower, I imagine the others' names: Larry will probably be something old-sounding, like Horace or Harold; Miranda will be, I don't know, Blondie maybe? I am sure Marco will choose something painfully obvious, like Jolly or Jingle. It occurs to me that I don't even know who the fifth person is.

By 11:30, everyone but Marco has assembled in the command center. Victor introduces the only elf I haven't met as "Raven. They/them." They look like emo-period Billie Eilish, an elf hat pinned back so that it doesn't hide too much of the neon green section of their otherwise dyed-black hair. Their eyeliner is thick, like they're an ancient Egyptian or modern Kardashian. This does not scream elfin to me, but that just improves my odds.

Victor has made us all change into new elf suits in jewel-tone velvets. Larry, who has selected the elf name Goofy, is in red, and Miranda, in gold, is now Buttercup the Elf, because *Princess Bride* is her favorite movie. Victor has chosen green for Raven, who has kept their own name, an idea that never occurred to me. I'm bummed at the color choices, because the green would have made my eyes stand out and because I *never* wear royal blue, which is what I get. Victor squinches up his face when I say I want to be Kodi, but he writes it down anyway.

Marco arrives, breathless, peeling off a bike helmet and accepting the purple suit Victor offers without complaint. From the dressing room, he calls out his new name: Jingle. (Nailed it!) And when he steps out to join us, I'm a little jealous to see that the purple looks good on him. I've got my work cut out for me if I want to win this, and he is target number one.

Santaland opens in about twenty minutes, so Victor explains that today's challenge is Meet the Elves. At noon, on the little bandstand in Santaland town square, a photographer will do photo shoots of each of us. With Santaland smack in the middle of the biggest wing of the mall, our audience won't just be the people in line for Santa time, but anyone strolling by on all three levels. That's kind of a horrifying thought. How will I focus on looking natural and likable for the camera when I'm wondering if, say, Leroy and his boyfriend are watching me from Zara?

Fiona appears, dressed as Mrs. Claus, all except for the wig. Her natural hair is tucked under a bald cap the same chalky white as her skin; a few tufts of red poke through, which makes her resemble a baby doll whose hair has been chopped off by an evil four-year-old. She is giving us some ground rules for the competition, but I can't focus on anything other than how much she looks like a prop in a horror movie. When she finally pulls her wig on, it's a relief.

"You kids have this all over me," says Larry as we leave the office to head for our photo shoots. "I've never been photogenic."

"You'll do great!" says Miranda. "Lots of grandparents come to the mall, and my mom says old people are the most reliable voters." I'm sure she's being sincere, but that's pretty hilarious. Raven and I share a smile; I may have an ally here. We could be like an alliance on *Survivor* and take down the others until it's just us.

As we enter Candy Cane Lane on the way to the village square, my heart stops: I recognize the broad shoulders of the helper passing out cookies to people in line. *Leroy* works here?

Oh man, this could be awkward. I envision the chilly silence that might settle over us if we're paired together. . . .

Or maybe it'll be great. I've been a little romantically challenged these last few months and the thought of snuggling into those arms again is pretty appealing. Maybe he and Shay broke up? Maybe it won't matter once he sees I'm back in town. But there's no way for me to know until he sees me.

As we elves file past, I try to catch his eye. I smile at him, and OMG, he smiles back. It hurts that he's so handsome. His walnut skin has always been perfect without any special regimen, and today it gleams. He swapped the long curls he had all last year for a fade that lets his eyes take focus. But I will always be the one who broke us up, so even thinking these thoughts feels a little wrong.

I play it cool, keep walking—it's the perfect casual start. But I can't help myself: I peer over my shoulder for one more look, and he's doing the same. He raises an eyebrow and laughs—*caught you*—and I am so happy at this turn of events that I trip over a giant gumdrop that houses a speaker playing "Santa Claus Is Coming to Town."

I face-plant to the words "so be good for goodness' sake."

"For heaven's sake, get up," Fiona hisses in decidedly non–Mrs. Claus fashion, and Larry and Miranda both reach for me, but Marco beats them to it, lifting me to standing all by himself. For a moment, he keeps an arm around me, until I shrug him off, embarrassed by the spectacle I have made.

I'm sure Leroy saw. Did the whole mall?

Raven stands apart from the rest, a half smile on their face, and I'm second-guessing my ally theory. Fiona adopts a cheery voice. "Come along, elves!"

Marco stays next to me. He leans in, whispering, "You okay?"

"I'm fine," I say, sure my cheeks are burning. "Thanks." The last thing I want right now is sympathy or attention.

I can't believe I came home to escape one debacle only to find another. I can sense that Marco wants to say more, but I just need a moment, and I stride past the other elves to the rotunda, trying to blink away humiliated tears.

I arrive first, Raven just behind. The good news is that the upper balconies—er, *galleries*—are pretty empty. Right now, the parents in line for Santa seem more focused on their kids than the photo shoot set, which looks like your standard school-yearbook setup: a plain backdrop, a stool, and a bored-looking middle-aged white dude waiting for us to arrive. The only hint of difference is a pile of giant sparkly candy canes that match our elf suits.

He looks up as we arrive and immediately seems less bored. "I get extra for retouching, you know." Huh?

Raven whispers in my ear, "I think he means your goose egg."

Oh my god. I touch my forehead, and I feel a lump that is *not* small. My cell phone is in my locker, so I can't use the camera app to look. I see a mirror in the photographer's gear and ask if I can borrow it; he tells me it's fine, but he'll charge me if I don't return it.

The shoot is in order of when we were hired, so while Marco starts his set, I am busy staring in the mirror at the mound of ballooning skin turning blue-purple. Call me Grape-y, call me Grimace, call me anything but cute, for I am going to be immortalized in mall history with a monstrosity on my forehead.

I hear whooping from the galleries and look up to see what appears to be a Marco fan club. Kids I don't recognize from school are calling his name and whistling. Marco is grinning back like nobody's business, and it makes him look really handsome. He's not even using the prop; it's obvious that his photos are going to come out perfect just as they are. When he steps to the mic and says, "Vote for Jingle!" I feel doomed.

More people are paying attention now, the cheering for Marco having drawn a crowd. When it's her turn, Miranda decides to put her candy cane to better use. She hugs it, and then she uses it like a microphone. And then she makes a choice that she is going to regret just about forever: she does a series with her lips puckered up to kiss the candy cane. She means it to be pretty innocent, but when teenage boys start yelling "HOT," it feels gross. She tosses the candy cane away, her face going scarlet. Laughter from the galleries sends her scurrying off the set, forgetting to introduce herself as Buttercup.

I'm not expecting much from Larry, so I use the time to scan the Santa line for Leroy. He's looking right at me. "You okay?" he mouths, and my heart melts a little, despite the exact same question irritating me when it came from Marco, like, five minutes ago. Should I mime that it hurts like hell but I'll live? Or, better still, should I act like it didn't faze me? I decide to do a little bow, and that's perfect. He smiles and winks at me.

Do I look as confused by this as I feel? He isn't acting like someone with a boyfriend. And I'm not acting like I broke up with him. If he's actually missing us, should I consider starting things up again? I mean, it's not like he ever hurt me or anything. At prom, I thought I was pretty lucky to be dating someone so cute and well-liked, not to mention someone who cheered on my talents (except for my singing).

But I *did* break up with him, and maybe not just because of the imaginary City Cam's imaginary boyfriend. If Leroy had a real hold on my heart, would I have traded him in for the future so easily?

When I look at the set, Larry's revealing a facet of himself I never saw coming: he's a comedian. He's using the candy cane to hook himself, while donning the wackiest expressions possible, his face seemingly made of rubber. *That's* why he chose Goofy! He leaves the set to loud applause. Ugh. He's real competition too.

Raven takes their place and tosses the candy cane out of the way. They stand stock-still, arms at their side, fists balled, lowering their chin almost to their chest. With head still down, they raise their gaze to look out from beneath furrowed eyebrows and the effect is demonic. They adopt a creepy, close-lipped smile and just stand in place, snap after snap after snap, swiveling their head slowly side to side to stare back at viewers. It's a genius look, somewhere between Wednesday Addams, Penny-wise, and the Joker. On the fly, they've come up with a real character that is unlike the others and yet kept their own name. Some of the parents are probably hating #Raven, but there is definitely a market for what they're selling.

What am I supposed to do? Nice, cute, funny, and scary are taken. As I drag myself to the photo set, I scan the galleries. Do I have any fans? I see Maureen Kropp, my old drama teacher, but she appears to be shopping, not watching. I look back at the waiting line; I see Leroy, and when I find him, he kisses two fingertips and taps his forehead in the spot where I have a goose egg on mine. Letting bygones be bygones, maybe? It's the sweetest. Bonus: his gesture gives me an idea.

When the photographer starts shooting, I palm my fore-head, a classic "Duh!" expression, which both hides the swelling and earns me a big laugh. I stay that way till I've heard a few clicks and that's it. I take a little bow to say I'm done, the photographer sputtering that I have to keep posing, but I don't. I walk to the mic, Kodi forgotten, and instead introduce myself as "Oopsy the Elf!" The kids in line all cheer.

The battle of the elves ain't over yet.

My coworkers/foes are scattered throughout the village, already on kid-wrangling duty, but Fiona has told me I can take a little time to recover from my fall. I'm staring at the contents of the first aid cabinet when I hear a voice. "I got you."

In a movie, I would turn around and discover Leroy standing there with an ice pack. The kind of perfect meet-cute that never happens in real life.

But this comes pretty close. Call it a re-meet-cute.

Leroy is holding a Coke Zero fresh from the vending machine. Gently, he holds the cold bottle against my goose egg. My mouth falls open—part from surprise, part from the delight of something cool against my throbbing forehead. The tip of his tongue touches his upper lip, a look he makes when he is concentrating really hard on his task.

"Wow," I mumble. "That feels great."

I reach up to take over holding the bottle, and our fingers brush as he hands it off. I feel the old spark. My tumble was the gift that keeps on giving.

"So, you're an elf? I guess that's a kind of acting."

I feel myself turning red. I shouldn't be embarrassed—I have to get used to this if I'm going to convince a season's worth of shoppers that I'm the best elf there is. And, I mean, he's not *even* an elf. Yet the acting comment still lands like a punch. He knows this isn't exactly a dream gig for me. "Just a seasonal job. Help pay the bills."

And then we are stuck there, him looking at me, me looking at him, a zillion memories in the air between us. The first time we kissed, on the flume ride at the Big E fair . . . the day I talked a friend who worked at Mickey D's (Leroy's favorite) into letting me man the drive-through window so I could ask if he'd like a prom date with his order . . . the way he held on to my hand for dear life at his granddad's funeral.

"Been a while," he says, cool and watchful. "Didn't expect you here." Leroy has always been a master of the short-sentence form.

"Didn't expect to be." I flash a smile that has a smidgen of apology in it. "But when I noticed you—"

"Noticed?" Leroy cuts me off, one eyebrow up. "That was some serious eye contact." He laughs, not meanly.

"Too much?" I ask, not sure what I want him to say.

He shrugs. "I'm back here, right?"

"What for exactly?" I say, not hiding that I'm flirting (boyfriend or no boyfriend). "Are you suddenly into first aid?"

"Sure." He grins.

And then he waits, expecting me to do the work. The thing about when we dated was that I had to lead all the time. I asked him out, planned most of our dates, was the first to say I love you, and the first one to suggest a sleepover, so naturally I was the one to lead the charge in ending things.

Remembering this makes me hesitate. Actually, it makes me want to break the spell. So I do. "Is your boyfriend into playing doctor too?"

Leroy's eyes flash. Sore subject, apparently. "We're taking a break . . ." he starts, then trails off. He steps back and gives me this annoyed look, or maybe a look that says he's remembering our split too.

I'm gonna have an empty photo frame in my room forever if I keep this up.

"Sorry," I start. But he doesn't let me get far.

"We're good." (It doesn't sound to me like we are.)

I haven't figured out how to reply when Victor comes in and sees us.

"You look plenty recovered," he snaps at me, and then eyes Leroy with irritation. "I don't recall you having a break scheduled an hour after the line opens."

Leroy isn't fazed. "Just being a good helper! I'll get back on the floor." And he's gone.

"Uh . . . me too," I say, not wanting to hang with Victor. "Where am I supposed to start?"

He squinches up his face, clearly wondering how he got saddled with someone so deficient. "Did you not even *look* at Elf Board?" (Um, no.) My eyes fly to what looks kinda like a crime scene wall, and I see that a royal-blue elf magnet is placed on the map by checkout.

"Got it." I hand him the bottle, knowing drinks aren't allowed in the village, and hurry away, glancing back to see Charlie Chaplin staring with consternation at a Coke Zero he never asked for.

Santaland closes at 8 p.m., but it feels like midnight at least. My feet hurt from standing in slippers all day and I'm a little rattled by a dad bellowing that the photo is not good enough to put on a Christmas card, so we should give him the digital file for free, which makes no sense. I try to sound reasonable. "I can't actually release the file without running a charge, so—"

"Swear to god," he booms, grabbing the register like he might throw it across the room. Releasing his grip, he stomps his feet and waves balled fists to protest the grave injustice of it all. His red-faced tantrum makes his four-year-old cry, and only the arrival of his mortified husband saves me. Apologizing copiously, dad number two scoops up their traumatized four-year-old, pays me for our most ridiculous package, and tells his petulant partner that if he wants a ride home, he'd better keep up.

Thankfully, he is the last customer—or *client*, as Victor prefers we say. When I get to the command center, Larry and Raven are both already gone, but Miranda and Marco are still here, watching a video on his phone. He waves me over to see, but I claim to be in a hurry and breeze by. It only takes me about three minutes to ditch elfwear for the cute outfit I barely wore today, but they're gone when I step out of the booth.

Only Victor is still at work, staring intently at a laptop screen. I don't ask what he's doing because I'm afraid he might answer. Instead, I try to sound cheerful as I say I'll see him tomorrow.

I get lost trying to follow the internal corridors back the way I entered earlier and finally just settle on the next door with an Exit sign. It opens onto a hallway with restrooms at the end of the Commons, which TBH looks just like any other food court. Unlike Santaland, the mall will be open for another hour, and there's a steady stream of traffic. Should I call it a day and go home—my feet would thank me for sure—or do I check out this supposedly wondrous collection of stores? There's that Zara I saw on my way in, the arrival of which has doubled my interest in the entire Pioneer Valley.

I see Leroy and his family heading for the new Cheesecake Factory in the mall and step behind a column to make sure they don't notice me. It stings a little because he and I used to make monthly pilgrimages to the one in Boston; honestly, I think the food all tastes weirdly the same and I find the gallon-sized portions a lot, but he loves it, so it was a big part of our year.

I don't want to look like a stalker, so I reverse directions, slamming directly into a tall slab of Christmas cheer.

"Cam!"

Marco, fresh from the Commons, holds a plate of seasoned curly fries and two corn dogs. He looks so happy to see me, as if I hadn't spent half my time avoiding him in Santaland.

He extends the plate toward me. "Want some? You didn't eat all shift."

I don't dare turn around, but I am hoping with all my heart that Leroy is seeing me with Marco, because I know how jealous he can be. If he thinks me and Marco are an item, he won't be able to resist the lure of competition. And I am more than happy for Leroy to try to win.

I lean into the moment, grabbing a fry with one hand while

resting the other on Marco's back. Happily, he doesn't flinch. If Leroy is even watching, we look cozy, maybe even flirty.

"You bought me a corn dog?" I ask, kind of amazed. (I hereby resolve to be nicer to him even if he is annoyingly chipper.)

He just laughs. "No. I always get two. I'm starved. But you looked kind of miserable."

"I did?"

"I saw you watching Leroy from Santaland—"

"I wasn't exactly *watching* him!"

"Okay . . . but I figure he's, like, an ex, right?"

I cross my arms. I don't love the idea that it was that obvious. "How could you tell?"

"I'm kind of a people spy," he says. (Are there other kinds?) "I watch and listen all the time, pay attention to all the little behaviors, the cues they don't even know they're sending." He looks so pleased with himself that I'm already fading on my promise to be nice.

"That doesn't strike you as creepy?"

"Nope. All the good writers do it."

"You're a writer?" The doubt in my voice is pretty hard to miss, yet he answers without a trace of defensiveness.

"I'm gonna be!"

"Are you an English major?"

His face clouds over. "Nah," he says. And he doesn't offer more, but I feel like I struck a nerve. He reaches for the plate. "If you don't want that corn dog . . ."

I hand the plate back. "I don't do fast food—I mean, if you

are what you eat, I don't want to eat all that crap." The words are out there before my brain processes that I have insulted not only the gift but the giver too.

He gives me this look, like *What the hell, dude?* and takes a huge bite of corn dog. "Good for you." He looks away for a moment and forces a smile. "See you tomorrow, Oopsy."

And for the first time since I met him, he doesn't sound happy at all.

Second Day of Elfmas

For a moment, I can't see. Kat Bizarro has ended up across my eyes like a sleeping mask. When I fling it away, the room is still dark. It must be pretty early, because my alarm—set for 8 a.m.—hasn't gone off. I'm not especially a morning person, so there's no good reason for me to be awake in the predawn Pioneer Valley dark. Just more time to wonder what the hell I'm doing with my life.

For the last few years of high school, I knew only one thing for sure: I don't belong in Lindell. For starters, I'm gay, which both is and isn't a big deal. Nobody's really hateful; even the jocks here are more like *whatever, dude*, but it's the kind of town where you (where *everyone*) can name all the queer people. You start to want more, you know? I dated Leroy my whole senior year partly because I had already gone on dates with Trevor and Loc, the other two gay guys in our grade, without either sticking. As for most of my teachers and classmates—they're all nice, right? But I get a little tired of being Encyclopedia Homosexualis for anyone trying to be woke.

New York has so many queer people, I knew I wouldn't be limited—not in dating, not in friendships. I could be gay without being an ambassador. But then I got there and felt almost old-fashioned for *just* being gay; when I admitted I'd never even considered girls, Sarah Xu asked me if I secretly hated women.

Theater, the other thing that Lindell accepts with a passive you-do-you shrug, was supposed to be my in. I had such a clear role in Lindell, pushing the club to swap out another production of *Sound of Music* (it would have been, no joke, the thirtieth) for *Urinetown* and then ending the stranglehold of musicals entirely by talking Ms. Kropp into an all-play season my senior year: *The Laramie Project* and a futuristic *Hamlet* set in a climate-change apocalypse. Some parents grumbled but we did it anyway, and the *Lindell Patch* said we "set the bar higher for all Valley high schools." Naturally, I wrote about this in my college apps—it showed me both as the serious actor I hope to be and as someone with purpose.

Aaaaand now I'm an elf.

Barring a Christmas miracle, the next two weeks will suck.

I grab my phone, which already has, like, a dozen texts from Jazz. The time is 6:32 a.m. What is the girl even doing up?

You better see this.

I tap the image, and it is my face. It is not my carefully

composed head-smack. Instead, whoever chose the official headshots for the contest picked an image that catches me, I don't know, midsneeze maybe? I don't remember sneezing, actually. But my lips are parted and one eye is half closed, while the opposite eyebrow is raised comically. The headshot graces the equivalent of a baseball trading card.

Oopsy the Elf

Age: 18

Likes: Silliness!

Dislikes: Boredom

Motto: I'm rubber, you're glue. What bounces off me sticks to you.

Tag #OopsyTheElf and #12DaysofElfmas and you could win a prize!

What the hell?

I leap off my bed and pace around my room. Is this supposed to be funny? They've taken my good attitude and turned me into pure comic relief. I text her a bunch of swearing emojis, but she replies:

Keep scrolling.

I realize I haven't seen the rest. It gets worse.

Someone has paired my trading card with a stunningly clear photo of my fall. #OopsyTheElf is joined with a new tag: #ElfFail.

The rest of Jazz's texts are versions of #ElfFail that are going around: the picture is edited so I am bellyflopped in a pool, soaring above Manhattan like a spaceship, or about to wipe out dinosaurs like an asteroid. Home less than a week and I'm a meme. FML.

I get to the mall an hour before my shift starts so I can find something fun to wear at Noche Buena, Tía Mari's annual Christmas Eve bash. I almost get waylaid by the cute-looking Biscuit Suprême bakery kiosk, but I make a mental note to come back later on my break instead. Maybe I'll invite Leroy—even though Tía Ely will be there and she isn't wild about him—and I want to look cute if I do.

Walking through the mall is surreal: Oopsy is everywhere. (The headshot, not the meme, thank god.) Not just Oopsy— *all* the elves. Individual posters framed on columns . . . all five on a banner stretched the width of the food court . . . even the information kiosks run the set on a loop.

#Raven looks like a horror-movie poster, the pose is so perfect. The #Buttercup image is the moment after Miranda realizes how she looked kissing the candy cane: her eyes are blinking in surprise and her lips are parted in a perfect O—it makes her look like an airhead. #Goofy looks a lot like the Disney dog—big open smile, eyebrows up—a half step away from a "Gawrsh!"

Of course, Marco—er, #Jingle—looks perfect. His broad grin is framed by those killer dimples, and I swear Victor has edited actual twinkles into his brown eyes. Is this rigged?

As for me, I can't tell if I look bonkers or like I was *trying* for bonkers. At school, I'd just claim I was committed to the character. But what exactly am I playing here? #Goofy has already captured the clown niche, so what does that leave me? The village fool? A walking disaster? If I'm lucky, at least no one will recognize me in street clothes. It helps that my goose egg has disappeared.

A text pops up on my phone. Sarah Xu. (She's one of those people whose whole name you say every time, like Elon Musk or Megan Thee Stallion.)

Sarah Xu, who hates my taste in music. Sarah Xu, who says my clutter "occludes her process." Sarah Xu, who once yelled at me for twenty minutes straight because I was late with my part of a group presentation. I was like, *chill*, but Sarah Xu has no chill.

Dean says you're not coming back. Seriously?

I'm not letting her gloat about having outlasted me. I delete the text and turn my attention to my latest obsession.

Because I'm a masochist, I've downloaded the 12 Days of Elfmas app, which has all five trading cards and a running ticker with the vote count.

"OPP-SY!" a little voice cries, mispronouncing the name so sweetly that I can't complain. A little girl in a red winter coat stands in my path. Pulling a Dum-Dum out of her mouth, she asks if she can take a picture with me. So much for going unnoticed. My contract specifically says no selfies in costume outside Santaland, but I'm not in costume. I kneel and pull out my camera and am ready to take the photo when she pokes me. "The face!" she says, nodding emphatically. "You have to make the face."

Oh my god. Is this my next two weeks? I do my best to mimic the expression I hadn't known I was making, and I wiggle the upraised eyebrow. This earns squeals of approval, and I admit, it feels kinda good. Sad that my adoring audience is under ten, but whatevs.

She takes a quick slurp of the Dum-Dum and then commands, "Now do *the fall*!" And just like that, the spell is broken. I tell her that it's against my contract and hurry away, hoping she's really bummed. (The little shit.) There goes one vote.

I'm surprised to find Marco at Zara. It's not that he dresses badly, just that I wouldn't have guessed trendy European to be his vibe. He's currently wearing a hoodie and jeans, practically the Pioneer Valley uniform, but cuter than I would have expected: the hoodie is in two-tone pastels, half pink, half purple, and it looks really nice with his pale ripped jeans and white sneakers.

I cringe a little, thinking of my exit last night after he tried to be nice with the corn dog. I can do better than that. "Nice fit," I say, joining him in line.

His look of concentration gives way to that smile of his. "Thanks!" he says. "You too. I kinda want that green sweater of yours."

The one I wore when I got the job? He *has* been paying attention. Then again, it's not like Larry or Fiona are burning up the style charts, so maybe I stand out.

"You like Zara?"

He grimaces. "Kinda, but the prices get me."

Nothing here is off-the-charts expensive, but the nearest T-shirt is fifty dollars, so he's not wrong. This makes me ask myself a question I should have asked before: Can I really afford to be buying new clothes for Noche Buena?

A manager walks up, holding a few sheets of paper. "Marco?" she says. "Let's take a look at your application."

As she leads him away, he mouths, "Wish me luck," over his shoulder, and I realize he hasn't come to shop at all. He's applying to work here, probably thinking about what happens when Santaland ends—something *I* should be doing too.

I could leave, but I don't. Instead, I try on a cool black-and-white party shirt that looks a little '80s and a little space age. It's on sale for the same price as that simple T-shirt, which makes my bargain brain say, *Buy it now*, even though my wallet is whispering, *Save yourself fifty bucks*.

Heading for the register, determined to shush my fiscal conscience, I see him emerging from his interview. "How did it go?" I ask.

"Great. I start January third, so no gap in pay!" He seems completely untroubled saying this, even though it's an admission that money is an issue. Money is always tight for me too, but I do everything I can to mask that by looking—and acting—like it's not. I wonder what it's like to be so up front about everything.

On impulse, I ask him if he thinks they're still hiring. Sure, working here would mean months more of his chirpy side, but cheerfulness isn't the worst crime, and I could use the employee discount.

His face lights up. "Yes!" He pulls out his phone. "Think how fun that would be!" He finds a QR code with the job posting and air drops it to me.

Standing there face-to-face, both of us looking down at our phones, feels a little like the moment you swap digits with a guy you meet at Pride or something. We both look up at the same time, and for a moment, I get a good look at his eyes, which are chocolate brown and incredibly expressive—the kind that get called puppy-dog eyes. There's a warmth there and an eagerness to please that is kind of adorable. For a half second, I'm like, wait—does he play on my team? But I know this glow isn't just for me: this is how he is with *everyone*. Seriously, it must be exhausting to be so nice all the time.

He breaks the spell by pointing out the shirt. "Are you gonna get that?"

"Well . . ." Now I'm not sure. It was kind of an impulse to come in, and maybe I should just hang it up.

"Try it on!" he says, more eagerly than the moment requires. He's not an employee yet.

I could tell him that I know my Zara sizing by heart, but something stops me. Maybe it's that I'm noticing how the hoodie hangs on his chest. Or how when he's smiling, his dimples are pretty cute. If he wants to see me in the shirt, why not?

A few moments later, I step out of the fitting room, and he circles me, admiring it.

"I vote yes!"

"Who says you get a vote?" I tease, and he pretends to be wounded.

While the clerk rings me up, Marco says he's going to get tacos in the food court and asks if I want to join him. I counteroffer, telling him about the bakery I passed. He shakes his head. "I need more than that. Haven't eaten all day. And it's a long bike ride here."

"No car?" I make it sound like that's a shocking scenario, despite the fact that I only have one because Dad is taking the bus while I'm home for break.

He looks away, and I get a feeling that this is a sensitive topic. "Don't need one." He shrugs. "I got legs!"

"*Yeah* you do," I say before I can stop myself.

What is wrong with me? "Flirt with Marco" is not at all on my to-do list. But he looks surprised—and maybe pleased? I try to pull back a little. "I mean, just, in your elf costume you can see your calves are huge"—this is not going well—"so clearly you exercise." This makes it sound like I'm checking him out when he's elfing. Please, universe—please let me off the hook. Maybe he didn't hear it the way it sounds to me.

But a sudden look of surprise changes Marco's expression. "You have something on your face," he says.

"Where?" I ask, grateful for the change of topic.

"All over," he says, a sly grin spreading across his cheeks. "It's kind of red. . . ."

Oh my god, I'm blushing! And he's mocking me for it! *Rude.*

I stride away from the cash wrap. "I'll see you at the command center."

"Cam?" he calls after me, looking mortified. "I was just playing—I thought—"

I keep walking, feeling the heat in my cheeks increase thinking about my lapse in judgment. Jaunty, smiley, happy, cheery—Jingle the Elf is *not* my type.

The elf profiles are the talk of the command center. I'm in the changing booth, listening to the others talk about their headshots. Raven thinks theirs looks too staged, an odd complaint for someone who just stood there looking creepy, but Marco assures them that it's perfect.

I step out just as Victor enters. He looks so proud of himself he might combust. "The impact is killer. Already twice the impressions of any other mall promotion since we opened. Instagram is especially hot. But we're trending on local Twitter and I saw a TikTok of a girl who can't choose."

Maybe he expects applause (okay, he gets it from Marco), but instead, Miranda steps forward. "You should have asked us to approve our headshots." Her lips are tight, and she does not look like a jolly good anything.

"Says who?" Fiona cuts in. "We chose the one that made *you* an ingenue. A babe in the woods. An old-school Disney princess."

"I'm not any of those things. I'm going to be valedictorian. I did a mission trip in East Africa. I'm—"

"A *character*. That's what you are. And you know who I am? A woman with a master's degree and limited tolerance for bullshit. Victor asked for characters, and I did damn well, considering what you gave me to work with." She points at Miranda, Raven, Larry, and me in turn. "Cutesy, goth, funny, a klutz—I made you as distinct as the seven dwarves and way more than the eight reindeer."

"What about me?" Marco asks, looking left out.

"Oh, well. You don't need a character."

"Huh?"

"You just *are*. You can't help it—you're like Christmas wrapped up in dimples. It's adorable." Even Marco can hear that this kind of praise is somehow also an insult, and he looks wounded. She tries to make him feel better. "No harm in being a completely nonthreatening pretty boy—you're Harry Styles in elf shoes." She thinks. "There are worse jobs than being the Hot Guy for tweens."

"Yeah," Raven says. "You could be #ElfFail."

"I saw that on Facebook," Larry says. He turns to Victor. "Are we allowed to do publicity stunts?"

"And post them?" Miranda pouts. "It doesn't seem fair if some of us do our own campaigns."

Wait—they think it's my idea? "Are you kidding? I didn't do that! #ElfFail makes me look like a huge loser."

Victor holds up an iPad. "A loser with followers. Every

#ElfFail post that also tags #OopsyTheElf ends up getting you a vote. You're in third right now."

Gathering around to see the stats is awkward. Marco is in the lead, of course, but Larry is right behind him, which actually is kind of shocking. Is Goofy really all that? Maybe it's the parents voting. I don't want to be petty, but the only thing worse than failing at being an elf is coming in behind someone older than my dad. I think I like reality-TV contests better from my couch.

Raven mutters, "Patriarchal bullshit," and stalks away. It hadn't occurred to me that the contest might make things uncomfortable around here. It looks like it hadn't occurred to Victor either. "C'mon, everyone. It's just a little friendly competition to keep things going. You'll get a Christmas bonus no matter who wins!"

Raven turns around. "Yeah? How big are we talking?"

"Big enough. Work every shift without a complaint filed by a customer—"

They smirk. "That's a low bar."

Victor nods. "—and the bonus is yours. So get to work." He points at the Elf Board and tells us to find our stations. Mine is "Collateral," which means all the other things you can buy aside from photos. It's a little gingerbread kiosk on Gumdrop Way, and we sell ornaments that, naturally, can be customized with the wallet-sized Santa photos, alongside toys that light up and spin, and, oddly, knockoff Elsa dolls, because nothing says Christmas like off-brand *Frozen*.

My first customer is a Korean teenager in a tee that says "SUPERFAN" but doesn't specify the target of her adoration. She has very round cheeks and dimples deeper than Marco's—like, deep enough to hide snacks in. "Playing Santa for yourself or someone else today?" I ask, quoting one of the many corny lines in the manual.

She laughs and laughs in helium squeaks, like this is the funniest thing ever. "You're hilarious," she finally gets out.

I have no idea what to say to this, so I quote my dad. "I've always been funny . . . funny-*looking*."

Her face changes in a flash, and she grabs my hands, deadly earnest. "Never say that again, Oopsy. YOU ARE BEAUTIFUL."

Okay . . . she's a little intense. I try to extricate my hands but it takes effort—she has quite a grip.

"Thanks?" I say, slipping behind the counter, so there is a fake gingerbread wall between us. "Let me know if there's anything else I can do for you."

The sunshine returns, her dimples double-dimpling. "Yes!" She sighs. "There's a lot you can do."

A white grandmother so pale that her veins are like rivers on a map leans over Superfan's shoulder. I've never been so happy to see an old person in my life. To my relief, I see a line has formed behind her. "Are you the only elf here? I need some help!"

I shoot Superfan a deeply apologetic look, one that clearly says, *An elf's work is never done!* And then I say to the customer doubling as my savior, "Santa does like his elves busy! How can I help you?"

Superfan steps away from the counter, but something tells me she won't be going far.

Santa duty is the best. His cottage has a faux fireplace that makes crackling sounds, which he sits next to on a giant love seat draped in furs and velvet throws. The lighting is all very flickery gold, which reflects in the frosted false windows. The mall music is absent, so you can hear the toy train clicking along its track beneath a crystal-decked Christmas tree, toot-tooting every so often. The quiet allows Santa to whisper to each child as if they are confidants—it's magic. All you do is steer children from the velvet rope up to the man himself and let him do the rest. Kids are at the happiest part of their experience—between the line to get in and the line to get photos on the way out—and the parents get two minutes to feel successful.

But each elf gets only ninety minutes on Santa, and today it flies by too fast. Every other job is worse. Two are traffic duty, one incoming and one outgoing, which really seem like helper jobs, but with the added burden of being the personality that is supposed to make everyone feel better while they wait. The worst job is photo elf, because you're the one who has to face parents with the finished photo, knowing the odds run about 50/50: either they'll coo about how it'll make the perfect Christmas card OR they'll start shouting that you, you personally, have ruined Christmas, maybe forever.

Fortunately, my turn on photo duty isn't up yet. I arrive at the outbound traffic lane to replace Raven, and I watch them do their thing a little. They have a whole shtick of acting like they are in cahoots with the kids, making eyes behind the parents' backs. The kids are eating it up and the parents seem happy that their kids are happy, but I wonder what will happen if Raven is ever caught in the act. Maybe it'll backfire, which would help me.

A frazzled-looking Indian woman wearing a quilted vest over her cream turtleneck is eyeing the arch above Smooch Hollow, a little photo op with a love seat beneath what are supposed to be bundles of mistletoe and holly. A boy, maybe three or four, clings to her legs. She tugs on a bundle of greenery, and it doesn't come off but it dangles loosely from the arch like it might. She turns to me, eyes bright with umbrage. "Are you seeing this? This could fall apart at any time!"

"I'll mention it to the Head Elf, ma'am!" I say in my most cheerful Oopsy voice, which is pitched a little higher than my own. "Maybe the reindeer have been at them!" I improvise.

"Are you making a joke?" The sharpness of her voice cuts the air enough to still the people in line. "Do you not take safety seriously?" Her eyes have become laser pointers of rage, and I am the target. How did this escalate so fast? My guess, based on her expensive Coach bag, is wealth; in my experience, privilege is like gasoline. "Do you want someone to get hurt?"

"Shit—of course not!" One pointed question and I've blown

my elf cover by swearing. I do what I've been told to do: I reach into my elf tunic for an Emergency Pop—or EP as we call them—a special rock crystal sucker that we keep to deploy when customers get rowdy. It's free AND shiny, two things people in a mall can't resist. Since it's not something you can buy yourself in the gift shop, its sudden appearance helps redirect attention for a moment or two. "I'll talk to the manager—Head Elf— right away," I say, trying to get my Oopsy back, and extend the EP, returning to script. "In the meantime, enjoy a special treat from the crystal caves of Mount Apology."

Okay, so following Victor's script might not have been the best call. She looks at me incredulously. "Really?" She snatches the EP from my hand and shakes it. "Which child should I give it to?"

I had seen the wide-eyed boy but not the girl, just about his size, standing several feet away, looking shy. *Crap.* I don't have two EPs. Marco had warned me that I should stock up, but Victor says they cost way more than candy canes, so he wants us to be stingy.

A dad in the now-snarled line calls out, "Can my kid have one too?"

Get me out of here.

"Sorry," I improvise. "It's like a lottery, kind of. Just one per elf! I'm out for the day now." I turn to Safety Mom and deploy a fake smile so big it moves my (real) ears. "Lucky you: you're the winner."

She narrows her eyes. She knows this fight is over and decides not to push it. "Tell the 'Head Elf' we expect a thorough safety review."

The command center's best feature is all the seating. Folding chairs, two sofas, even a giant office chair right off the bridge of a starship. I am so glad to sit down for fifteen minutes I could cry.

Victor rolls his eyes when I tell him about the greenery at Smooch Hollow. "Maybe it wouldn't be loose if she hadn't pulled on it!" He shakes his head. "If there's a nicer Santaland within a hundred miles, I hope she'll go find it."

"Right?" This is a good chance to bond with Victor, which I need to do if I'm going to convince him to give me next Saturday night off for Dad's Cookie Party. "And you should have seen her face when I offered her the EP. Like, she probably drove here in a Range Rover, and she's pissed I didn't have two."

Before Victor can reply, someone else does. "Um, I *did* see her face." Marco is in the door—which means my break is already up, sigh—and he's furrowing his brow. "She looked at the EP and then down at her kids, and I could totally see the problem. They're *kids*, right. They see this cool pop, and they both want one. What could she do? I felt kinda bad for her."

Wait—is this a Lecture the Elf station? I get his point, I do, but then I think of my dad taking two jobs and walking to work so I can have the car, and I just can't whip up much sympathy for this rich lady. And, honestly, Marco has already given me shit once today. I don't need any more. "Maybe she can buy them a candy store on the way home," I say over my shoulder as I head for Photo. So much for break.

To my very happy surprise, Leroy is the helper. We make a good team: I hand the families the packages and tell them how great the pictures turned out (even when the result looks like still footage of a kidnapping), and he rings them up. He flashes each customer a smile so pretty—there's just no other way to describe it—that I think it helps distract them from the cost, which is a *lot* more than it was when my dad was bringing me to see Santa over at the strip mall. One of Leroy's elf ears is kind of off-kilter and I start reaching out to fix it for him, but I have to fight the urge—we're not a couple.

I have to break the ice. While a burly dad fiddles with an overstuffed wallet trying to dig out his credit card, I lean over to Leroy and whisper, "What are you up to these days?"

I'm not expecting much. My guess is he's playing *Apex* with his brothers after school. Maybe cross-country skiing. What I really want is an answer that solves the mystery: Boyfriend or no boyfriend?

"Whatever I'm in the mood for." He shrugs. It's the least concrete answer I can imagine. "You?"

I raise open palms, the symbol for both "I don't know" and "I got nothing."

"I haven't been back long, so mostly just getting this job. I'll be home at least three weeks, though, so . . . lots of time to kill." I say this leadingly, because I know where I'd like to pass those hours.

Leroy and I spent the majority of our senior year together hanging out at his place; his dad's a contractor, and they have the nicest house in town, with a game room, a lap pool, a hot tub, and two living rooms (one of them sunken, with a state-of-the-art media wall). I *loved* his house—it felt like going on vacation to a really nice hotel—but I'm not going to invite myself over. If he has any sense at all, he'll take this as his cue.

And not just to invite me over. This time around, I want *him* to ask *me* out.

He looks like he might, but the customer produces his card finally and Leroy focuses on work instead of answering me. Three or four more families need assistance, including one whose giant, pimpled twelve-year-old should not be sitting on anyone's lap at this point.

When there's a lull again, our interrupted conversation hangs in the air. And finally the words are spoken: "Do you want to hang out tomorrow after work?"

But it's me who says them, my willpower apparently nonexistent.

"Yeah," he says, and our eyes lock. "What do you want to do?"

I grin a once-and-future-boyfriend smile, and he smiles back. This is going extremely well.

An older mom taps the register with her card to get his attention. "You boys"—she squinches up her face as she tries to phrase this right—"can *make merry* on your own time. But right now, you're in a—a *family* space!" We're meant to be shamed by this, but we both burst out laughing.

Last summer seems far, far away.

Maybe I'll get a Christmas miracle after all.

Third Day of Elfmas

I am awake with the birds—maybe before the birds—because of the text Jazz sent last night. I didn't see it right away because I was chatting with Leroy till one in the morning and planning our "first" date for after work today. When I finally saw what Jazz had written, it was a jolt.

If I find a second mustache, can Annika come?

That is a text only I would understand. Today is December 17, which doesn't mean a lot to most people, but does to Jazz and me. It's Wright Brothers Day, the day of the first airplane flight. We learned about it in sixth grade, and when it came time for a "famous Americans" project, we teamed up, me in a bowler hat as Orville and her in a mustache as Wilbur, in a mini musical, the best number being "Lord, Don't Let Us Crash & Burn." We've celebrated every year since, wearing the mustache and bowler out in public and pretending it's perfectly natural; we're always trying to top the location of the year before. Last December, we added period suits to the look and crashed a wedding reception at the Old Mill, this 250-year-old pub that people think of as romantic even though it now has a Cracker Barrel inside. Not only did they *not* kick us out, people took pictures with us.

Rereading Jazz's message now, I have two opposite reactions: I'm ashamed that I forgot all about it AND bummed that she wants to bring a date to *our* tradition. Color me hypocritical, but it seems wrong to bring a third wheel—December 17 is special! My conscience immediately reminds me that if it was really that special, I'd have remembered. And I have a date of my own already, so . . .

Now it feels complicated. I haven't been on a date in months, but I have this really swoony plan with Leroy for Birch Lights, a holidays-only illuminated forest walk a half hour north. It's really popular, so you have to buy timed tickets, which I did, using money I should be saving. I can't squeeze in a visit with Jazz beforehand; there's only an hour between the end of our elfing and the birch stroll I hope will lead to some serious making out in the woods.

I could just say I have to work and hope she'll call it good—I mean, it's true. Maybe she won't wonder how I'm using the rest of the night. But that feels icky too. She's my best friend—or was?—so I should prioritize her over a boy—even if he's a cute boy with skin so perfect he could be an ad for luxury face wash.

We could make it a double date, I guess. Sounds like Annika

is down for it already. But will Leroy be? He and Jazz are, um, not close. They always made nice when we were together, but Jazz thinks he's a little self-centered and she hated the way the relationship was entirely based on my efforts. She once complained, "He just gets to sit back and enjoy your affection," and she was not persuaded by my argument that I was just going for what I wanted.

Sensitive to slight, Leroy clocked her opinion of him early on without her needing to say anything. "What did I ever do to her?" he asked me once, serious. There was nothing I could do except tell the truth: Jazz has a very high bar set for who is worthy of her best friend.

At least they were never outright hostile to each other. With the added time and distance, it seems worth testing the waters again now.

> Just found out Jazz may be bringing her gf to Birch Lights.
> Total coincidence. Hope that's ok.

I see the ellipses that say he is typing. They start. Stop. Start. Finally, after I have aged like a hundred years, he replies.

> Cool.

I die a little. It's not a no, but it's not super enthusiastic, which is fair, because maybe he was envisioning a little snuggling too. I try to reassure him.

> We'll have time alone for reindeer games. Promise.

This time he replies faster with a GIF of two reindeer smooching. I heart it and decide to wait till later to tell him about the bowler (bowlers plural, now that I need two). He was never a costume guy, so I'm a little nervous about this.

I hop online to see if there are still tickets for our time slot. Wincing at the cost, I buy two more and text Jazz.

Surprise: I got us tickets for Birch Lights.

After a smiley face and a screaming emoji, she texts: Did you get 3?

FOUR.

???

I'll see your extra mustache and raise you a second bowler.

This occasions hearts, a fire symbol, and a few more screaming emojis. Damn. She thinks I met a boy. A new one. I better fess up.

Things are heating up with Leroy again.

There is a loooooong wait before she tags my text with a thumbs-up. She didn't say no, so I guess the problem is solved. Why don't I feel good about it?

Because one can never endure enough humiliation, there are now "12 Days of Elfmas" leaderboards at both main entrances to the Shops at Vision Landing. Essentially giant TV screens, they reveal that Marco and Larry are in the lead after round one. Their huge smiling elfshots alternate on a loop, with occasional flashes of Miranda, Raven, and me sharing the screen all at once like the also-rans we are.

The good news is that today's challenge is Story Time. I love telling stories—you might say I was born for it. The reading is happening just after the start of the shift, and I'm cool as a cucumber; seriously, this is my sweet spot. I'm tempted to do Rudolph, as a sly reference to reindeer games that only Leroy will get, but I choose *Memoirs of an Elf* instead, to be sure I stand out.

They have gathered thirty or so kids around the same bandstand on Santaland Square where we took the photos. As I enter Candy Cane Lane, a voice from one of the galleries yells, "Don't trip!" I can't help myself—I turn to see who it might be, but there's no way to tell. Looking over my shoulder means not looking where I'm going, and I bump into Miranda, who stumbles, and I have to help keep her from falling. "Sorry!" I whisper. Maybe it's on-brand for Oopsy, but I still feel foolish; I can just picture a blurry video of this moment captured on a cell phone.

She doesn't break stride. "You can't let them get to you!" It's really sweet of her to say that, considering I just about mowed her down. But then she overshoots in trying to rally my pride: "Remember—you're an *elf*!" Like there's any chance of me forgetting.

Raven goes first. They announce that they're reading *The Little Match Girl*. Naturally, they've picked the most depressing holiday story ever. I mean—spoiler alert!—it's about a girl who literally freezes to death, alone, on New Year's Eve. But damned if they don't sell it. They make this perfect sizzle noise every time the girl lights a match in the story, and whenever they recount one of the girl's visions, their eyes get so wide and bright, it makes me think that maybe Raven hasn't always been so goth.

Larry's rendition of *The Night Before Christmas* has me seeing him as a bigger threat than Marco: he does a killer Morgan Freeman impression, and the story is somehow richer and warmer than ever before. Miranda has chosen the nativity scene from Luke, and based on the blood vessels about to burst in Victor's face, I'm guessing she didn't warn him. He has made it clear that the mall's top brass prefers its Christmas without an infant savior in it, but Miranda doesn't seem to care, and she looks positively angelic as she talks about peace on Earth.

Marco picked *The Elf on the Shelf*, which I didn't even know came with a book. I thought it was just a creepy doll that moves around your house while you sleep to mess with your mind. The rhymes are all obvious and bad, but he sounds so eager and enthusiastic, it's hard to resist his energy. Even though he's my rival, I have to admit that his dark eyes literally twinkle—he's magnetic for sure. As boring as the book is, when the shelf elf tells the audience to blow him a kiss, not only do all the kids and parents comply, but from the galleries there are some decidedly non-elf-appropriate whistles.

This gives me an idea: I'll be interactive too. When my character says he wants to take an "elfie," I make a big deal of saying I left my cell phone at the North Pole and ask who wants to take one with me. Dozens of little hands go up, but I don't get to choose: Superfan from yesterday is pushing her way through the crowd and up the bandstand steps. She's really not what I had in mind, but I play along as she pulls me close for a photo. The crowd eats this up, so I try to stay cool and just keep reading. Near the end of the book, there's another elfie, and she yokes me once more with gusto. But this time, just before she takes the photo, she kisses me on the cheek.

Instinctively I pull away, looking shocked, and just as I do, a voice from the galleries yells, "OOOOPSYYYYY!" Superfan pumps her fists in the air like she has won a great victory, while the crowd whistles and cheers—well, all except Victor, who looks ready to burn down the village square. I race off the stage: the book might not be over, but this particular show is.

Ms. Kropp is in the incoming line with her niblings, as she calls her sister's kids. Draped in scarves because she is one of those white-lady drama teachers always draped in something, she billows like a sea when waving to me.

I'm not supposed to socialize with people while working, but I can't say no to Ms. Kropp. We both arrived at Lindell High at the same time, her first teaching gig after her gender confirmation at fifty, and me a freshman on the cusp of officially coming out. (Not that Jazz or my dad ever doubted where I was headed.) Not surprisingly, I link my coming out to hers, even if the two experiences are different. She's the fairy godmother every queer kid needs. And not just us—she's like an island for all the kids who color outside the lines of Lindell life in any way.

The last time I saw her was at my graduation, where she gave me a leather-bound journal to record the highlights of what was supposed to be my illustrious college career. I feel sheepish meeting her now in elfwear. "Probably not the stage you expected to see me on, huh?"

She claps her hands. "Au contraire. This Oopsy business is clever. It's nice to see you found your sense of humor again!"

Huh? "Did I *lose* it?"

"You know what I mean! You just got so *serious* your senior year—all Hamlet and Laramie all the time. You have such a natural gift for comedy!"

That *used* to be my brand. I could always get a laugh with an exaggerated look, a wacky voice, and, yes, sometimes an *intentional* pratfall. But that all seemed so *easy*. It was my shtick, not my gift. Let me tell you: I made sure there was no trace of slapstick Cam in my NYU application. I wanted them to take me seriously, which they did. And yet the end result might as well be the same: I'm playing a fool anyway.

"Well." I gulp. "I hope everyone else likes Oopsy as much as you. There's a big prize for the most popular elf."

"That is not news," she murmurs, digging around in her bag for her phone. She extracts it to open the 12 Days of Elfmas app. "You can only vote once a day," she says, "but be assured that I am."

I take her phone and see that the votes appear in real time, where I see that #Oopsy has now pulled even with #Goofy and #Jingle. Superfan actually did me a favor by creating a scene.

Handing back the phone, I turn the attention away from

myself and ask what the spring show will be at Lindell High. It's her turn to look sheepish. "Would you believe *Sound of Music*?"

"What? Why?"

"Not shockingly, the principal would like us to make some money once in a while." But then she throws up her hands. "And what can I say? I'm a sucker for swirling nuns and lonely goatherds and raindrops on roses."

"I thought you hated that show!"

She lets out a husky laugh and jabs the air. "YOU hated it. You thought it was so *beneath* you that nobody for miles would dare admit to liking it. Now that you're off to school, I'm up to my knees in curtain-hosen and it's heaven."

Note to self: never again have an opinion so loud that no one else can hear themselves think. I promise her I will be there opening night, ignoring the detail that I may not have far to travel for it.

"Ewww! Someone yakked on Frosty!" Behind us in line, a space has cleared around the famed snowman, whose white chest is now dotted with chunks of what is clearly neither coal nor carrot.

Thanking Ms. Kropp for the support, I dash over to help with cleaning up the mess. It's been maybe a half hour since Miranda said, with such pride, "Remember—you're an *elf*!" I bet she wasn't picturing this.

Yesterday, I took my fifteen but missed my lunch break while helping calm down a little boy who thought Santa looked like the scary walrus from some nature movie his parents now regret. Fiona was apoplectic about it, claiming that I risked earning Santaland a fine for breaking state labor laws. (Like, who would call this in?) Today she personally pulls me out of line to make sure I comply.

It's not the best deal: I have to change out of elfwear into street clothes, go grab whatever, and then return, eat, and change back in thirty minutes. The actual food court is at the far end of the gallery, so it feels like kind of a sprint. Instead, I go to the nearby Biscuit Suprême kiosk. Biscuits sound amazing. The girl serving has a white kerchief tied over copper-red hair and a scarf at her neck, which makes her look super French, an impression confirmed when she greets me. "Bonne journée! Bienvenue sur Biscuit Suprême." She pronounces the shop name "bis-kwee soo-prehm," and the kiosk instantly feels more luxe.

But when I go to order, I see only cookies. "No biscuits?" This comes out kind of plaintive, because I do love a good biscuit, and right now I'm so hungry I'd even love a bad one.

"Bien sûr," she says, fanning her hands out to indicate the selection. But then she lowers her voice to whisper, sounding totally local, "Cookies *are* biscuits. The name literally means 'giant cookies.'" I can tell from her tone that she's being helpful, not scornful. She looks around to make sure no one else can hear her. "Saying it in French is fancier, so they can charge more. You're an elf, so you know how it is." And she makes the universal sign of greed, rubbing unseen cash between her fingers.

The fact that she recognizes me is kind of cool and horrifying all at once. I did always want to be famous, though maybe not as someone who goes by Oopsy. But I appreciate her not mocking my complete lack of French, and I nod in agreement. I sigh. "A job's a job, right?"

I buy two "biscuits" and add a three-dollar tip, spending fifteen dollars, which is about the dumbest possible use of my cash in a week when my dad will be making hundreds of cookies I can eat for free. Sometimes I swear I am incapable of making good decisions.

But there's a silver lining. "Thanks for the tip," she says. "Maybe today I'll vote Oopsy."

"You didn't yesterday?" I tease.

She smiles. "Have you seen Jingle? That boy is cute!"

Ugh. What is it about this guy that makes everyone like him? Maybe they don't know how judgy he is behind those dimples.

I try to keep a smile on my face. "Yeah, but how does he tip?"

She laughs at this, and I pretend I think it's funny too as I head back to work, with fifteen fewer dollars, two cookies I don't feel like eating, maybe one more vote, and still no biscuit.

She's back! When I arrive at Collateral, Safety Mom and the children are in line, and she is holding up a spinning toy, eyeing it evilly. When she pushes a button at the base of an icicle, glittery snowflakes fan out like blades circling a glowing igloo dome at the top. "Does this seem wise to you?" she says to me specifically, as if I'm her own private elf.

Why is she here *again*? Based on the Coach bag and tasteful jewelry, I'm guessing she can afford activities for her children other than chasing Santa every day. *Whatever.* I take the offending object and bring it close to my face. As soon as the little rubber flakes touch skin, the spinning stops. "See: it's perfectly safe!" I say, and hand it back.

"Okay, now try it on your eye!"

"WHAT?"

"Try it on your eye. Go ahead."

"Who would do that?"

"A THREE-YEAR-OLD!" She raises the toy and shakes her fist at the cruel, uncaring universe.

"Don't blame the toy. Blame whoever's not paying attention to them!"

Safety Mom steps back, mouth hanging open, clutching the toy now like a talisman to ward off evil spirits. She gulps and then hisses, "Did you just say I'm not paying attention to my kids?" She raises her voice. "Did you?"

Oh lord. I have awakened the kraken. "No, no—not you, just anyone who would let a three-year-old—"

"Let? LET? Do *you* have a three-year-old?" Her daughter starts to cry at the raised voice. Mom's eyes are flashing with anger. "Do you have *two*? Because *I* do."

Suddenly Marco is there, brown eyes rich with concern. "Did somebody get ahold of a scary toy today?" He takes the spinner from her hand gently and turns to the nearest helper elf. "Can you put these all away until we can get a good look at them?"

Safety Mom softens. "Thank you," she says, the indignation fading away like contrails in the sky.

Marco looks at me, not smiling. "Take over Photos. I got this." I realize it's the first time I've seen his face without the dimples on display. Like a beach after a storm, the whole landscape is changed. He doesn't have to tell me his opinion for me to hear it loud and clear.

By end of day, I have fallen behind Larry and Marco again on the leaderboard, and Raven has pulled neck and neck with me. The five thousand dollars does not seem any closer, but at least I have my date with Leroy to look forward to.

I have just stepped out of the changing booth, and Marco is waiting, his expression dark. "What's up?" I ask, not sure I want an answer. Apparently, he has decided to use his words after all.

"You have to be nicer to people!" he says without even bothering to make small talk.

"I am nice!" I sputter.

"Maybe to some," he says, "but I've seen you on the floor, the way you roll your eyes. And you pick and choose which customers to help." Is Victor paying him extra to watch me? "And that poor mom today—"

"'Poor mom'? She comes in every day just to complain!" I fold my arms across my chest. I'm so not letting anyone defend Safety Mom.

"You've seen her, what, two times?"

"Twice too many!"

Marco lets out an exasperated sigh. "Okay, fine, but she doesn't need you shaming her. You don't know what her life's like."

"I wasn't shaming her! You swooped in at the last second, so you don't even know what I said. Who's judging who now?"

Fiona enters the room midargument. In her Bruins jersey and Timberlands, every trace of Mrs. Claus is gone. She doesn't ask what we're talking about; she doesn't care. "Clock out and go, will ya? I'm not a babysitter."

We sign out and walk wordlessly through the inner corridors to the exit into the mall. It's a relief to hurry out into the galleries away from Marco, but there is a prickly sensation up the back of my neck: I have the feeling he's watching me.

Dressing for an outdoor date is tricky because you want to look cute, but practical outerwear is *not* cute. This is New England, so it's going to be dark and cold, meaning I should wear the North Face parka my dad worked overtime to get me last year; it's super warm and waterproof too, but the cut is wide and the material stiff, so I look like a walking thermos. My actual favorite jacket is a knee-length car coat in black-and-white houndstooth. Based on the label and a little googling, I think it's from London in the late '60s. It's the one thing I own that felt cool enough to wear going out in New York, but it only took one walk along the Hudson to reveal that this coat is basically no protection against the wind. My choices tonight are freezing my ass off looking hot for Leroy, or staying warm and dull. Leroy will expect me to look nice, so my decision is made.

I choose the car coat, layered over a turtleneck. It really works with my charcoal velvet bowler, though it occurs to me now that Leroy probably did not choose his outfit with a surprise hat in mind. It wasn't hard to dig up a second bowler for him; my dad has basically kept every costume I've ever worn for Halloween, dance recitals, or spirit week. I grab the one I think will look cute enough; it's not as nice as mine, but it'll do for one night.

I wait in the kitchen, where Dad is baking World Peace cookies, which are little discs of chocolate with flakes of salt. They've been on the party rotation ever since he first discovered Dorie Greenspan, this pixie of a baker with amazing eyeglasses and a thing for Paris. She's like his baking guru at this point.

It's wild that he has probably two hundred cookie recipes at this point, but he does pretty much live for Cookie Party, which he's been doing since before I was born. Two weeks before the party, he starts making doughs you can freeze, and then he bakes a few trays each night the week of the event. He has a "how long" chart for the length of time certain cookies will keep and still be perfect. Prep is like a giant mechanical clock with all the parts calibrated so that the day of the party he doesn't make very much, yet when people arrive (also bearing cookies), there are at least a dozen varieties waiting, never the exact same spread two years in a row.

"What do you think?" he asks. "Is this year's hot one apple slippers or cardamom rolls?" One's French, the other Swedish; both he saw on cooking shows, and they're differently hard to make. Neither are as good the next day, so he makes one or the other as the very last step of party prep on Cookie Party morning, so that when guests arrive, the house smells amazing and there's a tray of fresh-from-the-oven treats.

"Cardamom," I say. "People love a warm roll!" Actually, I'm being selfish: whichever one he doesn't make for the party, he'll make for Christmas morning, and since I love waking up to the aroma of apple slippers, this is all about me.

Dad nods, pleased, as he slides the next pan of World Peace cookies into the oven. "This is why you should come home more often. Help me make decisions!"

Oof. He may have me home more than he wants soon enough. I try to tamp that thought down and distract him with my news. "Going on a date in a few. He's picking me up here."

Dad's eyes light up. "Tell me all about him! No, wait—should I put on a sweater?" By sweater, he means an ugly holiday sweater, as if the 3D Santa apron he's working isn't plenty.

"No." I laugh. "Leroy's seen your sweaters."

"I thought you broke up," he says, instinctively digging into the utensil drawer for two spoons, one for me, one for him, so we can share cookie batter while I spill the beans.

"Maybe we'll un-break things."

"Ah, the ways of love!" He nods sagely, like he has deeper

insight into romance than his spotty track record would suggest. I do know he's a softy. Dad and I watched *Call Me by Your Name* together, and it's kind of a lot to watch with a parent. There were some, um, awkward moments, but he cried so hard at the speech the movie dad makes to show his acceptance of Timothée Chalamet's character being gay that I thought for a minute Dad was going to come out himself. Really he's just an emotional guy—and it didn't hurt that this is, like, the most beautiful monologue ever written.

"I seem to remember that he likes cookies. Have you asked him to the party?"

The doorbell rings. Naturally, we have a programmable doorbell that Dad found on Amazon, and it currently plays the first bar of "Carol of the Bells."

"Let's see how tonight goes first."

Leroy is wearing a black quilted lodge jacket with a Canada Goose logo, which means he will be both warm and sleek all at once. His fade is tucked beneath a black knit beanie, which I hope he will replace with a bowler when the time comes.

I don't actually let Leroy in the house—Dad will never let us out if I do—just steer him immediately back toward the shiny black Tahoe he's pulled up in. The visible reminders of his wealth jolt me: Why exactly is he working as a helper elf? This I will ask later. He seems amused by the speed of our departure and waves over his shoulder at my dad, who is unabashedly standing in the doorway seeing us off.

In his truck (which really should come with a ladder), he laughs. "Couldn't get out of there fast enough, huh?"

"Uh—no—he's just, uh, he will grill you about everything you did the last six months and force-feed you cookies—"

"Your dad and the cookies." He shakes his head. "It's cute." He says the word "cute" lightly, in a tone that could be neutral yet tiptoes on the border of sarcastic. "He thinks you're still a kid."

Based on the crowd that fills our house every December, I'm pretty sure there's no age limit on cookie appreciation, but I play along. "I think he'd be happy if I stayed that way forever."

"Unlike mine," Leroy says. "He's more like . . ." He adopts a gruff voice. "'Grow a pair, Leroy. Be a man.'"

"How's that working out?" I ask, grinning, because I don't think Leroy is exactly the man envisioned by anyone with that voice.

"I took a job in tights." Leroy laughs darkly. "Just to mess with him." He falls silent and thrums the steering wheel for a moment. "And to stay out of his way." The subject of his dad has darkened things, so I turn on his satellite radio, which is playing Christmas pop. He lets his eyes drift to the hats. "What's with the hats?"

"Ahhhh. Yes . . ." I gulp. "You know I mentioned Jazz is going to Birch Lights . . . I actually forgot that it's Wright Brothers Day. . . ."

No recognition at all. "The tradition I told you about last year. . . . Bowlers? Mustaches?"

"Okay . . ." It's the vaguest possible answer but he also hasn't turned the car around to drive me home, so there's that. "If she's mustache and you're bowler, why do you need *two*?" He doesn't seem to be joking. I was *realllly* hoping he'd just get it, and I wouldn't have to say it.

"I . . . Well, I mean, Jazz's girlfriend asked for a mustache and I didn't know if you might want—"

"Oh." His voice stops me. He keeps his eyes on the road. "You know I don't do Halloween. . . ."

"Right, of course, I just didn't want you to feel left out—"

"Sure." He says nothing more, and I feel like I've screwed up.

To fill the void, I turn up the music. Ariana is singing "Santa Tell Me," and it's a bop. Almost at once, we both start dancing in our seats a little. Even sitting down, you can see that Leroy is a good dancer. For someone who can be a little tight-lipped, he's completely unselfconscious on a dance floor, and equally so bopping along to the rhythm here in the car. We're in the country now, the Tahoe gliding between snow-covered fields and old stone walls. Both of us are humming and grooving, and it feels so good, so easy, that I can't help myself.

When Ariana gets to "Oh, baby," I start singing along, full-throated, and Leroy winces a little. "I know you're not a fan of my singing. . . ."

"Nah, you're good." That may be the nicest thing he's ever said after I burst into song, and the fact that he's trying makes me want to reward him by shutting up . . . but not quite yet.

"Just till the end of this song," I promise.

"Cool."

Jazz and Annika, who is so blond her eyebrows sort of disappear, are indeed both wearing mustaches. They're holding hands and laughing at in-jokes as we stroll the shoveled path that leads into the woods, me in a bowler and Leroy definitely not. There's a real "one of these things is not like the other" vibe going.

I guess I'm not the only one noticing this. Leroy and I are a little way ahead on the path when he pulls me behind a giant evergreen to get me alone. "Are they gonna be with us all night?"

"Oh, uh—"

"'Cause I *thought* this was a date. Like, you and me."

"It *is*. Totally. I just forgot about Wright Brothers Day, and I didn't want to cancel—"

His eyes are narrowed as if he is trying to figure me out. He has every right to be skeptical, considering who dumped who. "It *is* a date," I repeat. "Trust me." And I pull him back onto the path as Jazz and Annika come around the corner.

If ever there was a time for "show, don't tell," this is it. When we come to the next fork in the Birch Lights path—a left route up a hill to a lookout, a right trail headed down to a pond—I wait to see which way Jazz will go. When she starts left, I grab Leroy's hand and tug him right. "Tell us how the lookout is. We'll be at the water." I don't give the girls time to join us.

Leroy keeps my hand as we head down a kind of slippery

path toward the shore. The slope is steeper than it looks at a glance, so we have to brace each other a little as we go. Leaning into him makes a warmth spread through my whole body. "This is more like it," he whispers. I couldn't agree more.

The trail ends at a pond maybe fifty yards across. Ice rings the edge for a foot or two, but most of the water is open, unfrozen, a black mirror holding stars in place. We could walk the perimeter easily, but instead, we just stand there, soaking in the beauty and the quiet. I lean against his shoulder and sigh, surprisingly glad to finally be alone with him again.

We turn toward each other in sync. And then our lips meet. His kiss is probing, as if asking questions, and I answer enthusiastically.

There is no easy way to keep a bowler on while making out, and soon he has kissed it right off me. I start to pull away to go after it, but he pulls me closer, deepening the kiss. I know I should be focused on Leroy right now, but velvet really shouldn't be lying in the wet snow. I wriggle out of Leroy's arms to retrieve it. "The hat," I explain, but Leroy looks unimpressed. "I can't lose it. My dad got it special for me in Boston. . . ." (Like everything in my life, it comes with a story.) I find where it landed a few feet away and scoop it up, brushing off icy crystals.

"Sure," he says, eyes shadowed. I'm pretty sure I've ruined the mood; fortunately, I know just how to fix that. I go back in for another kiss, bowler in hand, but before our lips touch, someone makes a loud throat-clearing noise. We spring apart.

An older couple who probably hadn't expected a gay pride demonstration on their holiday outing looks less than amused. Leroy doesn't reach for my hand as he heads back up the hill. But old habits die hard: I slip mine in his, and he accepts it.

Note to self: no costumes on the next date.

Fourth Day of Elfmas

Jazz meets me at Buzz—no Annika in tow—and when we settle into our favorite booth, it feels like old times for about ten seconds before she dives in. "Well, *that* was fun," she says. From her tone of voice, I know two things: "that" means last night and "fun" means the opposite.

Fine—let's go. "Right? What was up with you?"

"Up with *me*?" Jazz just about chokes on her matcha latte. "You're the one who ditched on December seventeenth!"

"Ditched *you*? You wouldn't even talk to Leroy. I peeled off so he could enjoy some of the night."

"Did you hear how he talked to Annika when they first met? He raised his voice, like she was deaf, or somehow managed to get into UMass without speaking English!"

I don't remember this at all, but I defend him like I do. "We were outside—he just wanted to be heard."

"'Cause Birch Lights is so loud. . . ." She rolls her eyes.

"I know he didn't mean anything by it. Not everyone is a natural communicator like you." This isn't flattery: it's a fact.

She softens and settles into her seat a little more, less braced. "I just was excited for you to meet her, you know?"

"She seems really nice—and I love that she wore the mustache all night."

Jazz grins. "Well, not allll night." She raises an eyebrow. "Your boy wasn't into the bowler, huh?"

"You know Leroy. . . ." I shrug. "Not his thing." I sip my iced coffee (yes, even in December).

"Then being an elf must suck."

"Worse—he's a *helper*. He has to wear the ears."

"I *almost* feel sympathy for him. That's new for me." She laughs. The atmosphere at the table feels like it's supposed to now. She fixes me with a look. "So, you're back together?"

"Well . . . I mean, based on that kiss by the pond . . ."

"But?" If there is ever a shred of doubt in my voice, Jazz will hear it, and has just now.

"I can't read him." There's no easy way to explain that his lips said one thing but some of his one-syllable answers said another. I think he's still holding the breakup against me, even if I'm trying to make up for that now. But maybe the bigger problem is me: I feel a little guilty for dumping him, only to start flirting with him the second I got home. I don't even know for sure whether I'm really into him again or if I just want him to be into me.

That much, I can admit. "Honestly, I'd like him to *say* he wants me back."

"Never gonna happen," she snorts.

Rena comes over wearing a Bruins jersey she's had for as long as I can remember. "Heard you were back," she says. The jersey, her voice, the whole thing makes my chest hurt a little. Buzz was my place here, and I haven't found that in New York yet. Who in the city would notice if I came back or not? "You doing okay?"

"Yeah, New York is great!" (Liar, liar, tights on fire . . .)

"Nah. In the little contest thing," she says.

"Oh, that." I grimace. "Third maybe? I have to step up my game."

"I voted for ya. But Steph is all over Raven. Likes all that goth crap."

Her wife voted for Raven? I feel kind of attacked. "But I'm a regular!" God, that sounds pathetic.

"At the hospital? 'Cause that's where Steph works." She chuckles. "Kid, she don't know you from Adam."

Jazz nods at this. "It's true, Cam. That's your problem: you have to win over everyone who *doesn't* know you."

"I'm trying!"

Rena snorts. "Yeah, well, whatever the next challenge is, try harder."

I'm on Reindeer Corral for my first shift, and Leroy is there with his little brothers in tow. They're cute, sort of, but a lot.

Like, *busy*. You never know what they're going to break or set fire to. It's not shocking that they're here, but I wonder why Leroy isn't in uniform.

"Did you quit?"

"Ha! I'm not an elf—I didn't sign away all my free time." He grins. "I'm a customer today."

"Yes, sir. How can I help?" I say in my Oopsy voice.

"You can start by paying attention to me." He says this in a joking voice, but I'm worried it's a dig about last night. But then he waves at his brothers. "To *us*, I mean. We'd like some reindeer feed, please."

The reindeer—with tags identifying them as Rudolph, Prancer, and, inexplicably, Trixie—are animatronic, so "feeding" them is pretty weak. The food of choice is Styrofoam packing peanuts, which end up piled into drifts that some poor helper will have to clean up later. The appeal is completely lost on me. I know, I know—a theater major shouldn't begrudge anyone their pretend play, but *still*.

My opinion is not called for; my job is to say "Let me help you!" with a big cheesy smile. I make a show of leading the brothers to the big bags of peanuts sitting in a bin marked "REINDEER FEED" in huge letters, and hand each a bag, instead of making them abide by Victor's "one per family" rule. "Nice," Leroy murmurs, and the boys look so happy with their bags, I have to admit that whoever thought of feeding plastic food to plastic deer may have been a genius after all. Leroy looks pretty pleased himself.

When they're distracted, Leroy whispers, "Trying to get my vote, elf?" And then he raises one eyebrow in the way he used to signal he really wants to go make out.

It's a relief to see that last night has not dampened his enthusiasm for me, but we're at work. "Um . . . put that eyebrow away."

He does not put the eyebrow away.

A clatter and crash from the corral makes us both look just as Leroy's youngest brother scrambles back over the faux wood fence, clearly having tried to ride Trixie, who is now flipped on her back, hooves pawing the air. Her big doe eyes are just the same as they were, but they take on a frantic look upside down, and her mouth, opening and closing, makes it seem as if she is gasping for air. Several children start crying, and I hurry inside the pen to "save" Trixie.

"Let me," says Leroy, and together we lift the reindeer. I make sure our hands touch as we settle the deer, even as I assure the kids that Trixie loves to play and she's having fun.

"Who knew this place was so dramatic?" I wink at Leroy, wishing I could find an excuse to touch him again.

"Right?" he says—him and the one-syllable answers! But he also winks before telling his brothers they've done enough damage. I wasn't lying when I told Jazz I couldn't read him. I just stare at him from behind as he walks away, as if this will somehow solve the puzzle, until the next kid asks for reindeer food and, once again, I point to the enormous sign they're old enough to read themselves.

When I get to my Santa's house shift, Miranda looks more than ready to hand off. Her eyes are wet, and her usual type A cool seems to be missing.

"You okay?"

She forces a smile. "It's fine. Thanks for asking." She does a little self-talk. "A lot of people have it a lot worse than getting yelled at by customers!"

"Who yelled at you?"

"This mom called me mean. And I wasn't, I swear."

Seriously? Her elf name is *Buttercup*. Who thinks she's mean? But then she points through the door to the outgoing line at a well-dressed Indian woman with two children.

"Oh my god. It's Safety Mom!"

"You know her?"

Santa clears his throat and motions me over with a velvet-gloved finger. When I am close, he leans in conspiratorially, his eyes twinkling. But the words that he whispers are anything but jolly. "Chat up the hottie on your own time."

(1) He is not my boss. And (2) *Ew, Santa.*

Old Saint Nick is messing with the wrong elf. "I'm pretty sure calling a teenage coworker a 'hottie' is a violation of . . . well, something."

"Jeezus Christ, snowflake."

"Like, I'm suddenly getting hostile workplace vibes all over. . . ."

He throws up his hands. "Just keep the line moving!"

"I'm sure Victor will have some thoughts." Stick that in your chimney.

When I return to the line, Miranda gives me a questioning look.

"I'll explain later," I whisper, and give Miranda a quick squeeze, which lights her up so that she once again looks like someone named Buttercup. She heads off to her next station, and I lead the next little girl, wearing a massive dental retainer, forward. While she lisps around her headgear that she wants a "dinothaur thleeping bag for Chrithmuth," I find myself gunning for Safety Mom and Santa; Santaland would be better without both.

I'm starved by end of day. Back in the break room, I open the fridge to find that Marco has left me a little box with the word #Oopsy on a yellow sticky. When I lift the Post-it note off, I see an expensive cookie from Biscuit Suprême and the message "Sorry :(" written on a napkin. It's signed "M." and I know that doesn't stand for Miranda.

Part of me feels guilty for reacting the way I had, but then I think about him telling me that I wasn't being nice to Safety Mom. When I put the two things together—him teasing *and* judging me—I don't feel sorry anymore. If somebody needs to be nicer, I'm not the one. And Miranda's run-in earlier proves me right anyway.

I change quickly so I can avoid Marco, and I'm successful. Larry enters as I put away my elfwear. "Got plans tonight, young man? Some gal waiting for you?"

First Santa, now Larry. How am I not obviously gay? I don't hide my surprise very well, and he adjusts. "Or some fella?" He smiles nervously and adds, "Or some *person*." And then he shakes his head. "Making small talk is harder than it was when I was your age."

Older people just can't help but show how much work it is to be cool. But cool is better than the alternative. "Nah. Tonight my date is with Dad!"

His face crinkles into a raisin of approval. "Well, look at you! And they say Gen Z is a bunch of brats!"

Keep trying, Grandpa. You'll figure out small talk someday.

I toss him a smile on my way out the door. Stepping out of Santaland, I witness a scene I did not expect: Raven and Miranda, arm in arm, heading for the mall exit. Senior year, in art history class, I learned about chiaroscuro, the contrast of light and dark. Raven's ebony mane and black leather jacket highlight the brightness of Miranda's blond braids and white puffer coat. My brain can't quite process the image. Jesus girl and the goth are friends?

Tonight is for Dad. I haven't really spent any time alone with him since my return. That's not entirely my fault. His job at the gasket factory (which I have never been to but imagine is pretty boring) is eight to three, so he leaves before I'm up. Five days a week, he comes home, eats leftovers, and then heads out to work a half shift at CVS. Saturdays, he only works at CVS, but a full shift. The only day of the week that he doesn't work is Sunday, but of course I was at the mall till eight. I should have spent that night with him, but I gave it to Leroy, because I'm an eighteen-year-old and dates are what I'm supposed to use my time for, right?

I'm making it up to him now. My dad has scheduled himself for fewer nights at CVS this week and taken the weekend off entirely. He does this every year, because Cookie Party is sacred. The financial loss stresses him out a little, but he's also the happiest he can ever be, so it's worth it. He says he has a new recipe to try out tonight, and I'm going to help.

He's in the kitchen wearing his favorite apron, which says "World's Best Mom." I got this for him with money I earned mowing lawns in sixth grade. It's a running joke because he's both Dad and Mom to me. I grew up knowing that the addition of a Y chromosome has nothing to do with changing diapers, doing laundry, getting me to drama rehearsals, or being the one who I cry to—and trust me, I was a crier. Still, when I looked at my friends' parents, he seemed a lot more like their moms than their dads.

After all, this is the life he chose. When I was little, he made it sound so natural that he was flying solo, saying he had known since he was a little kid that he just had to be a dad. The older I get, the more radical it seems that he did this. Sure, there were other single dads in the early '00s, but for a cishet man to go the surrogacy route—instead of holding out for the right woman to come along—made him kind of a unicorn. He admitted that he'd had his heart broken more than once, and he couldn't bear the thought that this might keep him from his big dream. "A biological clock," he used to say, "doesn't need a womb to start ticking."

"Aha," he says when I enter. "At last, my sous-chef is here." He hands me a recipe for Black and Whites, a cookie I've seen plenty of in New York, but he's never made.

It's a pretty straight up cookie, so it's not like he really needs my help, but the point is the company. While he lines cookie sheets with parchment, I get the music going. "Siri," I say, "play Ho Ho Homos." I started this playlist in eighth grade, tired of listening to the same carols over and over, and it's currently ten hours and forty-four minutes long. Initially, Dad was skeptical—the first song, "Joseph, Who Understood," is by a band called the New Pornographers and imagines what it was like to be married to someone who claimed to be impregnated by God. But he came around (a few Dolly Parton numbers helped) and now cues it up himself from time to time.

With Meghan Trainor crooning "I'll Be Home" in the background, Dad creams together the butter and sugar. I tell him about seeing Leroy and his brothers. Dad mixes in the buttermilk and flour as I tell him how I'm gunning for Safety Mom. He frowns a little. "What does that mean exactly?"

Honestly, I don't know. "Maybe I'll tell Victor she's harassing people. See if he can ban her. I mean, every day she gives somebody a hard time."

Dad is scooping up dough with our biggest scoop and turning the balls out onto the parchment, leaving plenty of room for them to spread. He flies through two sheets' worth, not commenting, and I can't tell if it's because he's thinking about what I said or just concentrating on making sure the cookies are uniform. Only after he slides them into the oven does he comment. "Well, be sure you know the difference between harassing and just being difficult. It's retail. . . ." He pauses and then shrugs. "The customer isn't always right, but they're not always wrong either."

"Uh-huh," I murmur, and change the topic. "I'll do the icing."

While I get to work, Dad swaps sides of the kitchen island with me, telling me a funny story about how his shift supervisor got locked in a bathroom stall. Listening doesn't distract me from the task at hand because it is impossible to screw up icing. There are a million ways to make it, but it always boils down to some combination of confectioners' sugar and liquid. This recipe also calls for corn syrup, I guess for the shiny aspect, but I add lemon juice too, as Dad taught me, to battle the sweetness overload.

The instructions call for a big batch of icing to be split into two bowls, the second of which will become chocolate once we add cocoa powder. But when I open the cupboard for the

Hershey's, Dad stops me. "Wait!" he says, and then produces a small bottle. "Surprise!"

He hands it to me, and honestly, I don't get it. I read the label and still don't. Purple food coloring? He refuses to explain. "Just mix it in and you'll see."

Okay, so I add a few drops to one of the bowls and immediately have a lavender icing. "Keep going," he urges.

I add a few more drops. The color deepens to violet. Oh no—

"Not Black and Whites—*Purple* and Whites!" he says, so happy it hurts. "Get it?"

I do: we're making NYU cookies.

"Once the basic icing has set, I'll do the little torches in purple on the white side," he says, describing the school logo. He's so damn pleased with himself right now. "These get the tower!"

The tower is this tree-shaped three-tier cookie tray that sits in the middle of the table to feature that year's special cookie. Pictures of the tower feature prominently on the Cookie Party spread of our annual family photo album too. We often refer to past years that way—"Oh yeah, that was the triple-chocolate-cranberry-oat party" or "Remember the blue halva year?"

The World's Best Mom is gonna be dialing 911 soon, because I'm about to drop dead of shame right here, right now, with Sharon Jones & the Dap-Kings singing "Big Bulbs" in the background.

Or I could just fess up. Tell him the truth and spare us the humiliation of erasing this cookie from both memory and the photo album later.

"Oh . . . NYU cookies!" is all that comes out.

He detects that I am not thrilled for some reason. "You can do the torch if you want—I didn't mean to hog the glory."

"No, no," I say. "You know you're better at the details than me. I just—" I just what? "I just can't believe you thought of this!"

He looks relieved. He leans toward me. "Would you believe I actually thought of them *last* Christmas? But you hadn't gotten your acceptance yet, so I held off. I've been waiting all year!"

Somewhere, there is a cruel-spirited god just laughing at me. I silently curse him or her or them but bury my discomfort. "God, Dad, you really are amazing."

Tonight isn't the night to reveal that *I* am not.

Fifth Day of Elfmas

Because there is a new challenge today, Victor has asked us all to come in early. (We better get paid for the time.) I already dropped my bag in the command center and hurried through the interior corridor past my favorite Elf Rule sign, which shows a big red ban symbol over a costumed employee flirting with a customer and the unintentionally masturbatory headline: "KEEP YOUR HANDS TO YOUR ELF." I snap a photo to text Jazz on my way to Biscuit Suprême, where I plan to order another overpriced cookie.

Honestly, I'm heading there in hopes that the ginger-haired girl is working again; I want to see if I can whip up a little support, now that I've checked the app. I don't know if we just have a lot of closet emo parents or if Raven has a ton of friends, but the *Little Match Girl* reading has brought them into a tie with Marco, with me and Larry behind them. Only Miranda seems out of the running.

"Bonjour, Oopsy!" she greets me.

"Call me Cam," I say, because it's bad enough being Oopsy in Santaland, much less outside of it. "But since you mentioned Oopsy . . ." Now what? "Do I have your vote?" OMG. Instead of subtly trying to suss out her opinion, I just turned into the worst politician in the world. "Sorry. Was that gross?"

"Yeah, it was!" She just laughs. "But I'd be gross too for five thousand dollars. If I had that kind of money, I wouldn't be speaking fake French and wearing this apron!"

I overcompensate for my gaffe by ordering one cookie for each elf, which makes her raise one red eyebrow. "You haven't won the five thousand dollars yet!" But she packs the cookies into a pretty little box, a purchase I know will eat a percentage of today's wages. Her eyes flash as she delivers good news. "And yes, I'm Team Oopsy, despite how cute your boyfriend is."

I don't follow. "You know Leroy?"

"I thought Jingle's name was Marco."

"Jingle? He's not—I mean, we're not a thing, at all." Where did that come from?

"Huh," she murmurs, looking skeptical. "In the competition, he can't keep his eyes off you. . . ."

"He has to watch *everyone*. You know, see what he's up against."

"I guess. . . ." She closes the box and seals it with an embossed sticker.

I'm not sure why it feels important to set her straight, but it does. "It's a lot more stressful than you'd think, being an elf." She slides me the box, nodding sympathetically. "At least for me, I'm paranoid about everything I do and say, and everything *they* do and say."

"That sucks." She offers a smile. "I'll work on everyone else here and make being Team Oopsy our thing."

"That would be amazing! Thank you!"

And then, without meaning to, she pops my bubble a little. "Just try not to fall down again. #ElfFail isn't your friend."

This I *know*.

Oh my hell. It's a *gift-wrapping* challenge.

When I was little, I watched *Queer Eye* on TV, and those guys were my idols. They could do everything—dress well, cook well, and make everything look perfect. Maybe it's silly, but I just assumed that was what being gay meant. And then I grew up to realize that I can cook decently from a recipe and dress with a point of view on the budget I have, but this is where my talent stops. My room isn't perfect or even especially neat, I don't have an interior design side, and the ability to beautify everything is not. My. Talent.

When it comes to wrapping gifts, I'm a mess. I'm congenitally unable to fold the corners into neat squares and diagonals. Patterns don't line up. Ribbons slide off at the corners. There's always some big wad of overflow paper that I wrestle down with tape, making the present look like it has a tumor. Maybe being more patient would help, but so far, I'm on track to never find out.

"The stage will be set with potential presents. Each of you will get to choose one roll of paper from the sleigh and one roll of tape, and you'll have ten minutes to convince the audience that you're the best wrapper. Questions?" Yeah, Victor, can I go home now?

Miranda looks as serene as I've ever seen her, so I'm guessing she's good at this. Raven raises her hand. "Are we all wrapping the same objects?"

Victor purses his lips, which really heightens the Charlie Chaplin thing. "God no. How would you differentiate yourselves? There will be objects of all shapes and sizes. Anything on that stage is yours to wrap, as many items or as few as you wish. The whole point is to make an impression."

Larry cocks his head. "So we could wrap twenty things really fast or one big thing really perfectly?"

Victor nods. "Whatever gets you votes."

Fiona adds her two cents. "We don't care: Make them all look terrible for a gag. Make them insanely complicated. Do origami. Just make an impression."

Naturally, it's Raven who asks, "Are there scissors?" It's a perfectly logical question, but from them, it sounds ominous.

"No. You'll use your teeth," Victor snaps. "Of course there are scissors. And the sleigh is full of ribbons and whatever else you need."

"And we're doing this live?" Larry asks, rubbing his head. Victor nods. "So why're we here early?"

Fiona and Victor share a knowing look, and some message passes between them. "We wanted you here together so we could tell you there's a little twist to the 12 Days of Elfmas."

There's something in the way Fiona says "twist" that makes my stomach clench. Blame it on the fact that I have seen every episode of *Survivor*, including ones from before I was born. (I applied for the show as soon as it returned from its pandemic hiatus and will apply again every year until they get a court order to make me stop.) I know in my gut what the twist is before she says it. Someone's going home.

"Today is an elimination round."

"WHAT?" Marco practically shouts, despite being just about as safe as an elf can be.

Victor chimes in. "It's purely a marketing thing—an elimination will raise the stakes. Engagement will definitely rise. We're already leading the mall in impressions, and this is going to go through the roof."

How on earth is that his defense? None of us care. We're here for the money.

"About that bonus . . ." Raven says, voice steely.

Fiona nods. "Just for making it this far, both elves will get an extra five hundred dollars. And you'll still be working, so your base earnings stay the same. Win-win."

"Both?" I sputter.

"Today's vote will take us down from five to three, and then we'll do another cut later."

The room is painfully silent, so Victor points out that we

still have jobs, ones with higher wages than helpers and most employees at the mall, and now a bonus of at least $500. "Come on," he says. "It's a sweet deal." But in case we don't agree, he reminds us we have signed contracts that we will work through the twenty-sixth. He doesn't say "like it or lump it," but it's implied. If I was a violent type, I'd put coal in his stocking and then lump him with it.

I may be the only one in school for theater—I don't actually know if this is true—but there is some serious acting taking place as we line up on the bandstand. Maybe twenty or so items before us range from the obvious (books, jewelry boxes, clothes) to the wackadoo, like the Prancer statue from the Reindeer Corral, a fully assembled crib on wheels, and a lawn mower. We're all smiling and pretending to make excited chitchat with each other, like we just stepped off the Besties Elf Train, but what we're really doing is preparing for the Ho Ho Hunger Games.

I feel Marco's eyes on me before I even look his way. When I turn toward him, he flashes me a big smile, apparently forgetting how he'd lectured me about my limited niceness. And then he winks. Could the girl from the bakery be onto something? I honestly don't think so, but to be safe, I don't wink back. I just toss him a perfectly harmless smile.

As promised, there is a sleigh onstage full of rolls of wrapping paper, bows, ribbon, raffia, pinecones, bells—anything you can imagine sticking on a package. A small table contains rolls of tape and scissors color-coded to our individual outfits.

I can hear Victor whipping up the crowd, which seems a little bigger today, but I don't process what he's saying. I'm strategizing: anything square is out, because me and precision are not close. It might make an impression to go big in my wrapping, but I can't be the only one thinking that, so it's a matter of deciding whether I can beat everyone else to the crib or lawn mower. Whatever we touch first is ours, so I could also—

The other elves are running before I even process that Victor has said *go*. Marco makes a beeline for the lawn mower, nearly tripping Miranda, who crosses his path on her way to the crib. Raven, much to my surprise, has chosen Prancer. All the eye-catching objects are gone, so I'm frozen, which is a really bad idea because it takes me a minute to realize that Larry is speedily collecting all the other items onstage—there won't be anything for me to wrap at all.

I grab the last unclaimed items, a coffee table book called *101 Places to See Before You Kick the Bucket* and a set of bath towels, my heart pounding because I know I have screwed myself. There is no way to make these "impressive," exactly, so I will have to earn a few laughs—once I figure out how.

Running to the sleigh, I choose the ugliest roll of wrapping paper I can—a hideous bright-green covered with photos of cat heads in Santa hats and the slogan "MEOWY XMAS!" in cartoon font. I grab the biggest bow in the sleigh—a red velvet monster the size of a basketball—and a handful of ornaments. I don't know what I'm going to do with *any* of it.

Claiming my scissors and tape, I set up camp at the back

of the stage so I can keep an eye on the others. Larry surprises me: he is an expert at this, wrapping every object with military precision. I mean, when this is all over, I want to barter some of Dad's cookies for wrapping lessons.

Raven is . . . I don't know what Raven is doing. They're just standing next to Prancer, spooling and unspooling the same long roll of black satin ribbon. No wrapping is taking place. And for that matter, they have no wrapping paper. Are they intentionally throwing this challenge? Maybe the bonus is enough.

When I look toward the lawn mower, Marco has it almost fully wrapped already, but he's chosen a white snowflake paper that is so boring, it's going to photograph terribly. I don't think this is quite what Victor has in mind. In contrast, Miranda has figured this challenge out: she is circling the crib at the speed of light weaving ribbon in and out of the slats of the crib like a textile expert. Alternating between green and red satin ribbons, when she completes one round, she starts the next above that. Five minutes in, she's already halfway to the top.

I stare at my finds. The book seems pointless, but maybe the towels could work? I think of YouTubes I've seen about cruise ships or beach hotels in exotic destinations and how they make swans out of towels. But then what? If I make a towel animal and then wrap it, won't that defeat the point? It'll just look like a lump. But I unroll my paper anyway, so I look active.

"I'm done!" I hear Larry say, and there he is at the front of the stage, with a dozen packages wrapped as if by the gods of precision. But it's not the perfect creases and flawless seams that take the cake: it's that, despite their various shapes and sizes, he has managed to stack them, biggest at the base to tiniest at the top, into a perfect tree-shaped tower, all tied in place with a green ribbon—in less than ten minutes. It's like seeing a black hole open up in front of you: it can't possibly be real, but your eyes assure you it is.

What do I do? WHAT DO I DO?

My complete inertia has gotten attention. "Elf Fail!" cries a voice from the crowd, prompting laughter as my face burns. I pick up a towel and stare at it, willing it to speak to me.

"Done!" Miranda has rolled the crib to the front, and it is majestic. She has used the slats to weave a gorgeous silk tapestry and topped off the effect with a green garland. It's not as technically skilled as Larry's, but it's more creative. You can see on his face that he knows this.

Marco is now rewrapping the mower—no, not rewrapping, but adding to the original. I get it: using narrower red paper, he's essentially turning the mower into a barber pole. And Raven? They just stand there.

Think, Cam, think.

I scan the crowd for a friendly face. The first person I recognize is Safety Mom, who looks, for the first time, not annoyed with me, but concerned, like she is witnessing a car crash. Beyond her, Leroy's face is completely blank. I try to make eye contact, but he looks away at that very moment. Was it intentional? I can't tell.

"Three minutes!" chortles Victor as Raven finally decides their time has come. They take the black silk ribbon, cut off a length, and tie it around their own neck like a choker, taping it into place. Then they tie a choker on the reindeer, unspooling the rest of the length as a leash. They drag the deer forward till they are next to Victor and yank the leash, so the reindeer topples. Raven steps on the reindeer's head, pretending to grind it underfoot, and snatches Victor's mic. "Who's prancing now?"

Victor looks torn. He's clearly horrified at the way Raven has turned into Dominatrix of Santaland, yet the crowd is raising the roof with noise: a mix of laughter, cheers, surprised exclamations, and boos. Everyone has an opinion—and if that's not making an impression, what is? The atrium echoes with *"Raven! Raven! Raven!"*

I feel someone watching me and, of course, it's Marco. He gives me a nod like, *Keep going!* But I shrug, resigned to losing. He shakes his head and mouths, "Just be yourself!" I have no idea what that even means in his mind, but it's sweet that he's trying to throw me a lifeline. Too bad I'll drown anyway.

"Two minutes!"

Marco turns his attention back to the mower. He has wisely left the wheels unobstructed, so he rolls it up to the front, where he receives pleasant enough applause—I mean, it's a red-and-white mower, right? But then he lifts it up over his head, and the inversion has the effect he was going for all along. "Candy cane, anyone?" he says, and suddenly the audience gets it. The applause grows louder; it might not be the star of the day, but his position seems safe.

"One minute!"

Be myself. Who is that? Cam the actor, or Cam the sort-of dropout?

No, not Cam at all.

Oopsy.

What if cookie girl was wrong when she said, "Try not to fall down"? Maybe that's exactly what I *should* do. Cam has no fans, but Oopsy does, and they have been clear about what they like: the tumble, the wacky face, the potential for one more screw-up. Letting go of looking good and leaning into the chaos of Oopsy-ness might just be worth $5,000.

I grab the wrapping paper and start winding it around my legs, somewhere between pencil skirt and mummification. I bind myself all the way up to my armpits and then tape it madly in place. The audience is eating it up, and Victor looks like I'm his personal hero. I make a giant oversized wrapping paper turban like a diva from a silent movie and finish it off with the bow. Only my arms are uncovered now, and I do what I can, unspooling the rest of the paper into a giant stole to wrap myself in.

Someone has started a countdown: "Ten! Nine! Eight! Seven!"

I have to get to the front of the stage without coming undone, so I hop forward.

"Six! Five! Four! Three! Two!"

The crowd is mine when they get to "One!" and I claim

my place in the lineup. I take a bow like it's opening night of a smash hit on Broadway. And, just as I planned, my costume splits wide open.

The crowd becomes a giant chorus of "OOOP-SYYYYY!"

One thing is clear: Nobody's sending me home. Not yet.

Today was a total #ElfWin.

Sixth Day of Elfmas

I'm up early, which is not like me, and I already have a terrible feeling about today.

Maybe it's because my morning started with another text from Sarah Xu.

CALL ME.

That's the whole text, and it's in all caps. A loud text from Sarah Xu is like an omen. The day is off to a terrible start.

In the shower, I think of how Leroy didn't meet my eyes when I was flailing during the competition. What was that about? And he didn't text last night, which is pretty bad boyfriend behavior—though I guess, technically, we're not boyfriends. We're still exes until we say different.

A blast of cold water hits me. You can't have two sources of water going at once in this house—running the faucet in one room means changing the water temperature and pressure everywhere else. Flush a toilet and whoever's in the shower gets scalded; start a load of whites in the laundry and all the hot water is stolen away, like it is right now. "Jeez, Dad!" I shout, trying to duck the icy spray. So much for feeling better.

I throw on a chunky Chris Evans–wannabe sweater and caramel corduroys. If I am eliminated, I can at least look cute at the mall while drowning my sorrows in biscuits. I throw myself onto my bed and look at the clock. It's not even 8 a.m.—today is going to be long.

I check the 12 Days of Elfmas app, but when I try to refresh the leaderboard, there's a pop-up message: "This Service Unavailable! Try Again Later!" It could be nothing, but it feels ominous.

I open Insta, and at first, all is good. Videos and screenshots of my self-wrap are everywhere, with tags like #VoteOopsy, #ItsaWrap, and #ElfWin. (I'm a psychic!) My favorite is #FailNoMore, and I could live off that all day, except there's another tag trending: #OopsyCheated.

The first appearance is late last night from a user named @XmasLvr. Their page is less than a week old, and #ElfFail is their first post—it looks like they may have started that trend too. Every story since has been about 12 Days of Elfmas, mostly sharing other users' favorable fan posts about Raven and Larry, with a few Miranda and Marco memes in the mix. With the new addition of #OopsyCheated, it's clear I alone am a target.

At first, I can't imagine any way that @XmasLvr could make the cheating claim. I used the wrapping paper, tape, and scissors they gave me. And okay, I was *thisclose* to too late but pulled it off just under the wire. It takes reading the comments to understand: Everyone else had followed the instructions to wrap the designated items, and I had not. The idea is that they were limited by working with what we had been given, while I just made up my own rules. Several posters argued that if the others had known it was a costume party, they too could have done things differently and it would have been a fair fight.

Ugh. I can lose even in winning.

I call Jazz for advice. But I get her voice mail. I try Leroy too, but no dice. Why would either be awake before eight on vacation? The only person I can bank on being up is Dad. Reluctantly, I head into the kitchen for his opinion, even though I know he'll just take my side. But he's already gone, having left me a note and two cookies like I'm Santa—if Santa had chores.

Cam Cam! Started laundry. Swap it over when you hear the timer. Please bring the trash barrels to the curb before you leave for work. Don't eat the apples—I need them for later. Love, Dad!

Naturally, the cookies he's left me are Purple and Whites.

I'm last to arrive at the command center, and the air is thick. Raven and Miranda, the unexplained duo, sit together on the sofa, while Larry paces. Marco is at the table with Fiona, but they're not saying anything. Victor is hunched over his tablet, swiping and scrolling like a fiend.

When I enter, Raven and Miranda look at each other, not me, and both stiffen. Larry comes to the table but doesn't take a seat. I'm at a loss—do I sit? Stand? Am I on trial or what?

"Hey," Marco says, the first (and only) elf to greet me, and he gives me a tamped-down version of his famous smile. His dimples are mere divots.

Victor clears his throat, looking up from the tablet at last. "The good news is that the Wrap-Off made more impressions than anything else we've done. Huge. I mean, huge numbers. And I don't think I have to tell you that Oopsy won this round big." His voice becomes aggrieved. "Un-for-tu-nate-ly . . . not everyone thinks this was a fair fight."

He reads some of the comments, one of which is "If you let this stand, it defeats the whole naughty-or-nice lesson and teaches children that Santa rewards even dirty little cheaters." (Honestly seems like a lot to put on my elf shoulders.)

Fiona rolls her eyes. "Somebody actually took the time to write that!" She practically snorts.

"So you're going to ignore it because you disagree?" Miranda asks. Everyone looks surprised except Victor, who seems to have known it was coming. Maybe she's the source of the complaint? "I think we should at least talk about it."

"Okay," Victor says, lips pursed. "Go ahead."

"Yes, it was funny, hilarious even, and I wish I'd done something like that, but you never told us we could skip the task—or just turn it into a costume challenge. I wouldn't have spent all that time trying to wrap the crib creatively if I'd thought I didn't have to wrap anything at all."

He seems to ponder this. "And what does everyone else think?"

Larry is first to reply. "I can see both sides, but it does seem like the boy's getting rewarded more for *not* doing the challenge than for doing it."

"Marco?"

All eyes fall on him, and he sits up straight. If he wants to eliminate me from the competition, this is his moment—he can take a clear shot. "Well . . . the rules were pretty simple: we had to wrap something onstage using the tools provided—"

Miranda cuts in, "Exactly!"

"And he *did*. The rules didn't say *what* we had to wrap. Cam was onstage and he wrapped himself, so . . ." Oh thank god: I have a defender. I give him a look of serious gratitude.

"Obviously *Marco* would say that," Raven mutters.

I don't see the logic, but Marco reddens. Raven reads my confusion. "You don't think it's his massive crush talking? *Really?*"

Whoa. Sure, he's brought me food. Okay, twice. But we barely spend time together, so when would this have happened?

Marco's face is beet red, but he doesn't protest. I'm speechless, so Larry fills the void. "Now, I don't see how this needs to get personal like that. Either Cameron followed the rules or he didn't."

Now we're all looking at Victor, but he narrows his eyes and turns back to Miranda. "And if I say Cameron broke the rules, what are you suggesting I do?"

Miranda kind of hunches inward, becoming smaller. I don't think she expected the boss to put this on her. She sounds a little miserable as she offers timidly, "No points from the Wrap-Off?"

"Whoa!" Marco looks shocked.

Victor nods, considering this. "So the idea is that if he didn't wrap one of the objects, he didn't really complete the challenge. . . ." She nods warily. "And no challenge equals no points." He adopts a rueful expression. "I guess that applies to Raven as well, then."

Raven sits up straighter, one dark eyebrow cocked.

Miranda blanches. "Why Raven?"

"Can we really say Raven wrapped Prancer? They tied a leash on a reindeer and dragged it across the floor. . . ." Ooooh. Good point.

He turns to me. "You've been quiet. What do you think: Did Raven wrap anything?"

My jaw drops. Is he really making me answer? "I—"

Fiona is loving this and speaks over me. "That would make it so easy. If two are disqualified, we have our top three."

Miranda gasps and grabs Raven's hands. "I didn't mean to do that. I swear. You have to believe me."

Raven pulls their hands away and folds their arms. "I told you complaining wasn't a good idea."

"I take it back!" Miranda pleads to Victor. "You can't take their points."

"But I should take his?" He knows he has her cornered.

Miranda groans softly. I'm betting she's doing the same calculations I am: if I keep my points, the likelihood is me and

Marco will be safe, meaning there's no chance she and Raven *both* can make the top three. Finally, she throws up her hands. "Fine. Let it go."

"Are we agreed?" Victor asks, and Larry nods his assent. Marco looks relieved, and Raven does too, surprisingly, even as they comfort their defeated . . . friend? Girlfriend? (Is that even possible?)

"Okay, then, we stand by the votes, which have now been counted. With yesterday's numbers, the five-day totals are clear: Marco, Raven, and Cam, you're still in the running to become Top Elf. We'll do a little reveal at the bandstand in a few minutes, present some giant fake checks for Miranda and Larry—don't worry, you'll get real ones too. We'll tell everyone to keep voting since the race is so tight—"

"Is it, though?" Raven isn't playing.

"See for yourself," he says. "You have the app."

"It doesn't work," I say.

He waves dismissively. "That was this morning, when we were dealing with cheating-gate. I froze it so no one could mess with things." He taps and swipes. "All set now."

Marco and I both lean over Victor's shoulder to see. Marco is still in the lead, but Raven and I are in a dead heat not impossibly far behind him.

There's a tug on my sleeve, and when I turn around, it's Miranda. She looks nervous, her blue eyes wet. "It wasn't *personal*. I just . . . We needed it. And I tried so hard."

I feel her disappointment in my bones. I know how sad

I'd be right now if I had lost so soon. I open my arms, and she accepts a hug. It feels good, honestly. And then Marco is hugging us both, his arms warm and strong. "Group hug!" he calls out.

"I am not doing that," says Larry with a laugh.

Raven agrees. "That makes two of us!"

Word has gone out on social media that today two elves will be cut. The crowd seems larger than ever, and I wonder how it is that all these people can be free on a Wednesday afternoon. There are definitely more stay-at-home parents or work-from-home employees than I'd ever have guessed. I feel a little nervous, maybe because some of them are probably in the he's-a-cheater camp.

Victor's eating up the attention. "With the most votes and the top position, elf finalist number one is JINGLE!"

Lots of cheers and, from the galleries, some stomping, which makes his reception thunderous. Marco's smile is just about big enough to split his head into a flip-top, like a Canadian on *South Park*. He takes a deep bow and then, working the crowd, winks and blows a kiss. The audience eats it up.

"Our second elf finalist is a dark horse . . . or maybe that's just the goth talking. RAVEN!"

It doesn't make sense to me, but it seems the ones cheering loudest are little kids. (Though a group of college girls from the galleries comes close in volume.) The youngest ones seem to love Raven, which means maybe they just understand kids better than I do. Or maybe they're just more like a character from a cartoon than the rest of us. Whatever it is, Raven is a hit.

Fiona comes forward with the two big checks, the names of the recipients covered. "The two eliminated elves will each get a little extra stuffing in their stocking," she says in an adorable granny voice nothing like her own. "Five hundred dollars." The crowd applauds as if they're the ones getting the bonus prize. "And they'll be here through the twenty-sixth, so you can still meet your favorite!" She passes the mic over to Victor. "Back to you!"

Glancing over, I see Larry and Miranda are both keeping their cheerful faces on, as if they don't know what Victor will say next.

"We've had some lively internet debate about our remaining contestants"—it's a ridiculous statement; everyone knows he means *me*—"and after a thorough examination of the rules and extensive consultation with the judges"—who do not exist—"it has been determined that they are *all* eligible for the last spot."

There's no ignoring the boos—a few float down from the galleries and several parents in line look dismayed—but his announcement generates decidedly more applause. In fact, the crowd seems to know what's coming, because he can't even finish the line, "Elf finalist number three is . . ."

"Ooooop-syyyy" is already filling the air, a long call-and-response that echoes through the atrium.

I see Leroy in the crowd, and this time he meets my eyes. He flashes that smile of his, and it's a relief. His smile . . . the crowd chanting my name . . . it doesn't get better than this.

My shift flies by. All afternoon, kids and parents are excited to meet me. Because it's hard to take compliments without deflecting, I keep explaining what a bad wrapper I am, and it's amazing how many people say they feel the same way. Victor is right: people really are into this competition, and at least right now, it feels good.

I don't need to bust out an EP to calm anyone down today; there's not really any drama until I encounter Safety Mom again at Photo. Her little boy is chanting "Photo! Photo! Photo!" quietly but very intensely and she shakes her head no. "Are we ever getting one?" he asks, face scrumbled into a pout.

"Not until they take a good one!" she says. "They keep snapping the shot when your eyes are closed."

I am standing at the register and can see the display. She's mistaken: the children are both smiling, eyes fully open, and looking beautiful. I'm about to show her this, but when I lift my eyes, she catches me looking and gives a tense little head shake, as if to say, *Do not help.* Hmm. Maybe she's not Safety Mom at all but Cheap Mom. The bag might be Coach, but nothing says it's recent. Whatever it is, I play along. "Next time, we'll do better!" (By now it's pretty clear there will be a next time, as she goes for the record of Most Visits to Santa.)

Before they exit, she turns to look at me over her shoulder, and I see something I didn't expect: a mix of wounded pride, gratitude, and exhaustion. Interesting.

★ ✳ ★

In the parking lot, I see Raven lugging Miranda's check, and I try not to look too curious as I wave goodbye to them. Larry is parked right next to me, and I tell him I'm sorry it didn't work out. He waves it off. "You know I'm doing this for fun, right? Keeps me outta the house. My grandies—I got eleven—think it's pretty cool to see Pops on TikTok and whatnot." He leans toward me conspiratorially. "I don't need the money. I'm a retired general, air force, and trust me, I got mine. You kids knock yourselves out over the cash."

With that, he gets into his car and pulls away, leaving me marveling at how little I knew about him. I'm about to back out of my spot when Marco raps on the window.

"Congratulations!" he says, eyes sparkling.

"You too," I say. And something comes over me. I suddenly want to know if Raven is right. More than that, I realize, I kinda want the answer to be yes. It's silly—I mean, I don't even know if he's into guys, let alone me. And I have Leroy already. But something about Marco is hard to resist, despite my best efforts. "I . . ."

I what?

"I . . . like being an elf with you."

Oh god, the things that come out of my mouth. Yet he doesn't seem to care if I sound like a dolt. His whole face glows. "Awww! I like it too!"

It's starting to snow, lightly, but it feels like a gift from the

· 126 ·

gods. "Do you want a ride? I bet we can fit the bike." I assure myself that I am not flirting, just being a decent coworker.

He hesitates. "I don't live close. . . ."

"All the more reason," I say, and we wrestle the bike into the back seat.

As we pull out of the parking lot, I put Ho Ho Homos on the stereo, and he immediately starts singing along. Not with polish, but joyfully. He seems, um, indifferent to the actual key but still makes it sound good. I join in, and we try to outsing each other until we are howling. The ride home really is like jingle bells: we're laughing all the way.

I'm still on a high when I get home from dropping Marco off. My house is not very big, but you can hardly tell this time of year, because of how much it glows. Dad wrapped the house in colored bulbs (you can't be surprised he's not a white-bulb guy), and the lawn is covered with inflatables. Tía Mari says it makes no sense to pinch pennies all year and then waste all that money on an electric bill at Christmas, but I don't know how anyone could begrudge Dad this. Mr. Christmas to the core, I think he draws on his holiday battery for energy the other eleven months.

This year, the centerpiece is a sleigh pulled by winged hogs—when pigs fly, get it?—and a giant Olaf from *Frozen* but with a pride scarf. There must be a leak in Olaf, because he's gone a bit floopy; he's bent over like he's barfing, which is hilarious and gross all at once. It's unlike Dad to let this sort of thing slide, but I decide to be a good son and solve the problem myself. The issue is that the opening connected to the blower is loose, letting out air—which is so easy a fix, even I can do it.

Entering the house, I call out, "You're slipping, Dad! I had to save Olaf myself."

There is no answer. You know how in a book, somebody says "the house is too quiet" just before discovering a body or something? The house is too quiet. "Dad?"

I find him at the kitchen table. Just sitting there. Trays of unbaked cookies sit on the counter, looking forlorn. His eyelids are so heavy, his eyes are almost closed; the laugh lines are transformed into crevices of worry. His cheeks are pale, as if the color has drained away. He looks so tired.

"Dad, what's wrong?"

He doesn't answer me, not right away, but he also doesn't look at me. He tries to but can't lift his eyes.

Oh no. No, no, no. My grades must be up. But how would he know? The great perk of college is that your parents aren't supposed to know anything you don't tell them.

"Sarah Xu . . ." He can't say it.

My first thought: my roommate's dead. My second is nearly as bad: she called again, and now he knows about school. The hurt in his eyes tells me it's the latter.

"I . . . I . . ." And suddenly I'm crying. I slide into a seat and put my head on the table to just let it all go.

"You . . ." He is crying too and doesn't go on.

"I don't know how I screwed up so badly."

"... *lied to me.*" The way he chokes this out kills me.

"No—no—" What do I say? "I just only told you the good stuff."

The look he gives me, the one that says he can't believe I'm going to argue technicalities right now, makes it even worse. "You can't talk to me now?"

I say the truest thing I can. "I'm ashamed, okay!" I get up from the table and stalk around the kitchen. Snowmen with their cheerful ceramic smiles mock me from all directions. But it's easier to face them than my dad. So they get the whole confession.

"I didn't fit in—and I didn't even know why. Everybody else just seemed to know the things to say and what to do, and they all got it. But it was nothing like what I imagined. Or . . ." And this is the part I have trouble admitting even to myself. ". . . what I wanted. I just shut down. Not everywhere—I mean, I liked my gen eds, but my theater classes—I was so sure I didn't belong that I guess I just . . . *proved* it. By the time I realized I was failing—"

He looks baffled. "*You* failed classes?" He's never been a dad to a kid who failed anything, so his surprise is fair.

"Well, I think so. . . ."

"'Think so'? You don't even know and you're planning to drop out anyway?"

Pulling out my phone to log on to my student account gives me something to focus on other than the stricken look on his face. And when I open my grades, it's my turn to be surprised.

"Show me," he says, and I do, still trying to process what I've seen.

"One B, one C, a D, and an I," he reads. "Does I mean incomplete?"

I nod, amazed; my stage combat teacher has done me the biggest kindness ever by giving me a chance to finish.

Dad's wheels are turning. "Does the I count toward your GPA?"

"No—not till I finish the work." How exactly will I make up stage combat homework? (Beat myself up maybe? That I can do.)

He sounds more hopeful. "This is a C average, then. No need to quit . . ."

I hate to break the news. "It leaves me below the minimum GPA—"

"For your scholarship," he says. He is silent a moment and then waves that fact away. "I don't want to talk about the money right now. I want to talk about whatever I did to make you feel like you couldn't trust me."

"It's not about you!" I shout. Why do parents have to do that—take everything you do and trace it back to them being good or bad or whatever? I mean, I'm the one who dreamed of going to NYU only to discover I can't hack it. Can he imagine how disappointing it is to know that you signed up for a long, expensive mistake and have no backup plan?

Dad reels back, surprised at my passion. His eyes flash in a decidedly non-Christmas-light way. "Oh? I'll remember that at the plant tomorrow, and I'll remember it again when I get to CVS."

Considering I literally just shouted at him, he had good reason to clap back. But it stings. He has always said not to worry about the money, and even though I knew better, I told myself he meant it. I get up from the table, feeling light-headed.

"I thought you wanted me to go. I thought you supported my choice. If I had known you saw it as such a *burden*, I would have gone somewhere closer or cheaper, but no, you said, 'Follow your dreams, Cam-Cam, go for it.'" He looks like I've slapped him. "Maybe I didn't tell you because I knew you wouldn't be able to handle it. And look at you! Guess I was right."

Dad gulps. "Cam!"

"I'm going to bed." I head for the stairs.

"Cam-Cam—" he offers weakly.

I should turn around. Or he should follow me, make me face him. One of us should say something. But we don't.

#SonFail. #DadFail.

Fail.

Seventh Day of Elfmas

This is new. I have a text from Victor, which contains a link to a spreadsheet and instructions. Today's challenge is—thank you, gods—a bake-off. We don't usually know the challenge in advance, but I guess it makes sense to tell us, since Victor needs to order all the ingredients. I have this in the bag. As a kid raised on Cookie Party—

Cookie Party. Dad. Last night.

Ugh.

I turn to my patron saints, Ryan and Emma, dancing on the wall, and ask them to give me wisdom. But they keep their eyes on each other and ignore me.

The news that I haven't flunked out leaves the door open to going back to NYU, even if my scholarship is gone. I'm not good at math, but I can add and divide just well enough to calculate that even an A on my incomplete won't push me to a B average. That means it's Top Elf or nothing if I want to go back.

I don't even know if I do. But it's better to have a choice than not.

Maybe the bake-off is a double win: it gives me something to talk to Dad about—if I haven't already missed him. Still wearing my jammies—okay, a Harry Styles concert tee and silk boxers I swiped from Leroy and never gave back—I race down the stairs.

He's just finishing up a note for me and about to head out, but I stop him. "You can't leave yet! I need the whoopie pie recipe." He doesn't respond out loud, but gets down the notebook he keeps his favorite recipes in. He hands it to me, open to the correct cocoa-stained page, which features multiple versions of the cake-like sandwich cookies with their frosting filling.

I fill the silence by explaining that I need this for the Elfmas bake-off, not that he asked. "Everyone around here loves whoopie pies, right? So that's a safe bet. But they're not Christmas cookies, so people won't expect them. I'll use the *red velvet* recipe but go easy on the cocoa and dye them green instead of red, then stack them in the shape of a Christmas tree."

Dad nods. "Sounds good, Cam." That's it. He gives me a kiss on the cheek and is out the door, leaving me gobsmacked. Quiet Dad is the worst Dad. He's hurt or mad or both and if he's not *saying* so, it goes deep. Well, that goes both ways. I'm still hurt too. Maybe he wrote an apology in the note.

Going straight to CVS from the plant. Order takeout. Love, Dad.
Ouch.

★ ✴ ★

The bandstand looks like *The Great British Baking Show* meets a prize package from *The Price Is Right*. There are three ovens upstage, arrayed in a half circle; downstage sit workstations, each with KitchenAids, food processors, cooking tools, and dry ingredients. A hefty fridge hosts all the perishables.

"What fresh hell is this?" asks Raven, first to arrive at their station, holding up an apron adorned with Rudolph's face, complete with a 3D red plastic nose.

Mine isn't much better: it's shaped like a snowman and has a really phallic carrot sticking off the front. Marco, as usual, is late, and all I can see on his apron is a Christmas tree; I'd bet good money it lights up. In comparison, he's getting off easy.

Victor is nowhere in sight, but Fiona explains that we'll have thirty minutes to get our recipes made and in the ovens. Easy enough. Once things are baking, we're supposed to work the crowd, like the mini celebrities we now are, until our respective timers go off. We'll be back onstage for assembly of our creations, which will be presented to the crowd and then taste-tested by ten lucky audience volunteers and a "mystery judge."

Victor arrives at last and makes a few announcements of his own. He's hired a half dozen new helpers because the crowds have really picked up and he wants us elves to be free for promotional opportunities when needed. "Right after the bake-off, you all have interviews," he explains. "You'll still be on the floor some, but you're not just anyone now—you're mall royalty, and we want to milk it."

"Mall royalty?" Raven says, their eyes just about rolling away inside their head.

"Interviews?" asks Marco, a little nervously. "Someone's writing about us?"

Victor sweeps his hand toward Smooch Hollow, where a camera crew is setting up equipment. "*Filming.* Christa Delcamp from NBC is doing a feature on the competition. It's human-interest catnip. Just make sure to give them a good story about what you'll do with the money!"

Christa Delcamp is my dad's favorite. He watches the early morning news before the factory, and he says he can just tell she's a good person. She has this cat-who-ate-the-cream grin that makes her kind of impish, and when she laughs, which is not infrequent, he laughs too. I can't wait to tell him about this . . . assuming he's actually still speaking to me.

From a distance, I see an unexpected figure, Shay, at the edge of Santaland. I don't see Leroy, but why else would Shay be there? They did break up, right? Am I being paranoid or petty? I don't have time to indulge either.

Miranda and Larry join us at the bandstand, Miranda trying to sound cheerful as she announces that the pair are our designated sous-chefs. Larry jokes, "Help out? Fine. But trust me, you kids don't want me cooking anything."

Fiona tells us we need to take our stations, and as we do,

Marco passes by (apron now lit up and twinkling) and whispers close to my ear, "Can I get a ride home again? Last night was fun." And he smiles a smile that could melt a snowman.

"Absolutely!"

Victor explains the challenge to the audience and tells them about the filming, but I'm stuck on Marco. I kind of wish he hadn't whispered anything; he's away at his station, but the electricity of his closeness is still radiating through me. I know I should focus on my whoopie pies instead of checking him out while he bakes. Maybe it was a ploy to distract me—if so, it's working.

Ringing a strand of jingle bells, Victor tells us to go, and we start. Sifting together the flour, cocoa powder, baking soda, and salt is effortless—I've done it a million times. I cream the butter and brown sugar together, the KitchenAid doing all the work for a moment, which gives me time to watch the others. God, Raven is a weirdo. They're cracking eggs, very slowly, one at a time. The whites go in their mixer, and the yolks end up in the trash. (That oughta smell nice later.) There appears to be nothing else on their table. It looks more like performance art than baking.

And Marco? *Whoa*. I have no idea what he's making, but it's purple. Like, really, really purple. It makes sense, I guess, in that it sort of matches his elf color, but I don't know what it has to do with Christmas. What I do know is that he appears to be talking or singing to himself as he works. It's clearly helping him concentrate on whatever grape extravaganza that is. (I hope Victor wasn't expecting cute trays of gingerbread men from this group, 'cause we are *not* delivering.)

I get the eggs and buttermilk I need from the fridge. I mix them with vanilla and add them to the dry ingredients all at once, yielding a batter that is perfect in texture. I need only whip in the food coloring, and I'm all set. I asked for gel instead of liquid because it's more dramatic and—

Where is it?

There's no food coloring, liquid or gel, on my table. And it's not like there's anything for it to hide behind. I fairly stomp to the fridge, trying to imagine who thought food coloring needed to be refrigerated, but it's not there either.

Victor and Fiona are nowhere to be seen, so I call Miranda over. "Have you seen the food coloring?"

She cocks her head. "Marco's? It's not exactly food coloring but an extract or something."

"No, *mine*! It's green." I move my phone to show her my list. The line for "green food coloring, gel preferred" has a checkmark like all the rest, which means somebody bought it. So where is it now?

I think about the sudden appearance of the #ElfFail meme and then the online campaign to paint me as a cheater. And now this? Color me paranoid, but @XmasLvr—or *somebody*—is sabotaging me. Why? *Who?* I scan the crowd as if that will help.

"Snap out of it!" Miranda barks, and I am startled. "Do you want me to look for it or not?"

I hesitate. Somehow, I have burned up twenty minutes of my time. "Yeah . . ." I say. "I can use it in the frosting if nothing else."

Forced to adapt, I put in the full amount of cocoa used in the regular recipe. The dough takes on a rich, chocolaty color, which normally would make me salivate, but I'm scrambling for ideas on how to make this more interesting. If she doesn't find the food dye, these will end up just being old-school whoopie pies. How am I going to win with that?

I glance at Raven, who is standing next to their mixer, which is now whirring away at high speed. I see a clear frothy liquid and still don't know where this is headed. They look a little bored.

Miranda comes back empty-handed, this time with Fiona as Mrs. Claus in tow, as if she needed backup to tell me that there is no food coloring to be had. Not bothering with her Claus voice, Fiona says, "The receipt shows we bought it, so you must have lost it."

"Lost it?" My head pounds. "*When?* Did you see me scoop up ingredients and go for a jog? I literally have been nowhere but here."

Looking sweet like Mrs. Claus but sounding like a boss with other things to do, Fiona tells me that's a shame. "Guess this makes it a *challenge!*" she says, and leaves me to scoop my now-boring dough. I thank Miranda when she grabs me parchment to line the cookie sheets with, but I can't help wondering: Did *she* do this? She's acting all helpful now, but who's to say she's not doing everything she can to take down Raven's competitors?

Raven is using a pastry sleeve to pipe batter onto their trays, and I realize they're making meringues. From here, the meringues appear to be plain white, which is good—we can be equally boring. Marco is spreading the startling purple batter across his pan like a very thin sheet cake. Maybe he's doing a psychedelic Yule log?

My whoopie pies are in the oven well before Victor rings the bells to call time. Raven is right behind me with their sheets, with Marco last, sliding a single pan into his oven.

As soon as I'm released, I make a beeline to Victor to complain.

"How am I supposed to do anything if I don't have all my ingredients?" I snap. He fixes me with an acid look.

"I didn't take this job to be your personal shopper or a crisis hotline. Solve the problem. *After* your interview." And he turns on his heel, leaving me to fume. No, he's leaving me to pretend I'm not fuming while I head for Smooch Hollow.

Raven is already there, on camera, and Marco is watching with interest. I can't wait to tell him about my missing food coloring, but Leroy steps into my path. "Congratulations, top three!" I can sense that he wants to kiss me, but we're at work, so that's a no. He hugs me instead.

"Thanks," I say. It feels nice in his arms, and yet I'm conflicted.

It's only been a few days since our date, but Marco has changed the temperature of things a little. Leroy is every bit as beautiful as ever, and a big part of me wants him to go in for the kiss, but there's Marco just beyond Leroy's shoulder, and for the first time, I realize I want to kiss him too. I am apparently a fifteen-year-old in spring again—all hormones.

Leroy follows my eyes to Marco and his own widen. "There some elf-on-elf action going on here?" He drops the hug.

"No!" I say, maybe a little too loudly.

"Good," he says. "'Cause I thought we were back."

"Are we? I was hoping . . ."

"You weren't sure?"

"I kinda wanted you to ask."

He raises an eyebrow. "I shouldn't have to."

It's hard to explain why that bugs me, but it does, so I push back a little. "I guess. But, you know, I did all the work last time. I asked you out the first time. . . . I was the first to use the word 'boyfriend.' . . ."

"And the one to break us up." He has a point. But so do I.

How did we get from congratulations to stalemate so fast? I don't want to leave it here.

"I'm sorry," I blurt, which isn't 100 percent what I'm feeling, but it does the trick.

"Good," he says, and gives me a quick kiss. "I'll see you tonight."

When I join Marco, Christa Delcamp is still talking to Raven. "Why is it so important to you to win?"

Raven looks at the camera, not Christa. "My sister is my best friend, and maybe the only person in the world who gets me. She can't win now, but I can, and if I do, I win for both of us!"

I look at Marco in amazement. "They're siblings?"

He looks back at me, differently amazed. "You didn't know?"

"No—I just—They're so different. I thought Miranda was all religious—"

"She is. They're Latter-day Saints."

"RAVEN is a Mormon? Looking like that?"

Marco frowns. "I guess their folks aren't exactly thrilled about it, but Miranda says they love all their kids the same—there are six, I think. . . ."

"*Six.* Whoa . . ." I remember what Miranda said about needing this win, and now I understand. "I bet the money would come in handy."

"It would for anyone!" he says as a cameraman motions him over. Christa helps him find his mark.

Raven comes to join me. I tell them I didn't know they were related to Miranda. "Yeah, I'm kind of the sore thumb in my family. But Miranda's kind of the sore thumb at school, so we watch out for each other." I apologize for never asking more about them, and in typical fashion, Raven doesn't mince words. "Yeah, you seem pretty Cameron-focused most of the time." But they let me off the hook a little. "But maybe it's a good strategy: easier to crush an enemy you don't know!"

I feel a tap on my shoulder and turn, hoping it's Leroy coming to make up, but it's Superfan, who is now, to my horror, dressed in helper attire. Oh my god. There will be no escape.

"Look!" She beams. "I work here now."

"Oh . . . wow."

She takes this as enthusiasm and extends her hand. "I'm Kandy, like candy cane but with a K."

A light bulb goes off. She has inadvertently saved me. I burst out, "Oh my god! I could kiss you!"

She stops, not so much happy as puzzled. "Oh? Wow. I don't think we're supposed to—There's, like, a poster—"

"No, sorry, I just—You just inspired me. I know how to finish the challenge now!"

Her face is aglow with pleasure. "Make sure you thank me!"

But I can't solve the problem yet. The cameraman is steering me toward Christa, who I hear telling Marco how touched she is by his story. (Which I don't know. Because I never asked. Raven is so right.)

Marco winks at me as I take the spot. Christa is a tiny human being in person, a ball of electric presence radiating you-got-this. "So, tell us about yourself—real and elf!"

"My name's Cameron Ceballos—"

Someone in the galleries yells "Cam!" and I wave, though I'm not sure who it is.

"But at Santaland I'm Oopsy the Elf." This is greeted with a chorus of elongated "Oooop-syyy"s. "I'm eighteen and have lived in Lindell my whole life. I . . ." This part is tougher to say. ". . . study theater at NYU and hope to be an actor someday."

I see Ms. Kropp in the crowd, nodding encouragingly, and feel a pang: I'm not the only one who will be disappointed when I drop out. I almost miss Christa's next question. "What's been your favorite part of the 12 Days of Elfmas so far?"

"Not being eliminated?" That gets laughter from the crowd,

but I'm surprised to find myself answering seriously as well. "The people. Larry and Miranda and Raven and Marco— they're great to elf with." The audience likes this answer, and I feel pretty good about how I'm doing.

"So why do you want to win? What would that mean for you?"

It never occurred to me that I would have to out myself as a failure. My chest constricts. I can't. I can't do it. So, I tell half the truth instead. "My dad is a single dad. He works two jobs to pay the bills and . . ." My voice cracks. ". . . let me go to college. I'm doing it for him." Thinking about last night makes me want to cry. "He's the best, even when I don't act like I know that."

Christa looks at the camera. "I hope you're watching, Dad— that's quite a tribute!"

When the camera stops, she tells me she loved my answer. I tell her she's my dad's favorite anchor, and she flashes that smile he loves. "You probably tell that to all the anchors you meet!" But she takes a goofy selfie with me to send him—he'll be in heaven.

Larry comes to tell me that everything is out of the oven cooling and that we can return to our stations for the next round of prep. I ask him if he can do a mission for me: grab two dozen candy canes from our elf stash and bring them to my table.

Back on the bandstand, Raven has two trays of meringues cooling and has pulled up a chair to sit, reading a paperback copy of *Flowers in the Attic*. I know there must be more to their cookies—Raven is stealthy—but so far, the results look unimpressive.

I start mixing my frosting. True whoopie pies use marshmallow fluff as the secret ingredient in the filling, and that's what I do. But I'm not finished until Larry brings me the candy canes. I use a butcher knife to chop the candy canes into bits the size of sprinkles and save half. I put the rest in the food processor, crushing them into a sparkly red-and-white powder, which I whisk into my frosting.

Marco has frosting of his own, which he is spreading across his purple cake. As I suspected, he's making a log of some kind, carefully rolling the cake from the end of the pan so that the colors make a pinwheel at one end. No idea what it is, but it's pretty eye-catching.

It's time to assemble my whoopie pies, making sandwiches with two little chocolate rounds on either side of the now-minty frosting. I make the filling twice as thick as usual so that there is a lot of cream exposed. I lay the chopped cane bits on a tray and roll the cookies across it, so that the frosting picks up the candies. In an instant, ordinary whoopie pies become bedazzled with holiday cheer. It's not green, but I still stack them into a Christmas tree shape, because *cute*.

A jingling signals it's time to put up or shut up. Victor leads ten audience members onto the stage, including Safety Mom, followed by Christa Delcamp—the perfect mystery judge. I don't see her going all Gordon Ramsay on the contestants.

Fiona appears in full Mrs. Claus mode. She comes to me

first. "Tell us what we have here, dear, and why you made them."

I'm not about to say that I made them because someone stole my ingredient. I raise the platter with my cookies. "My dad and I are big whoopie-pie guys, and I learned to make them when I was, like, ten. But my other favorite cookie is Girl Scout Thin Mints, which I do not share with my dad or anyone else—get your own box, right? So, I put the two things together in an *original* recipe"—I slip that detail in for whatever points it might get me—"that I'm calling Peppermint Bark Whoopie Pies."

There are plenty of oohs and aahs and a smattering of applause, but I can't tell how big a response I've gotten. I'll need to see how they react to Raven, who ignores Ms. Claus's question and addresses the kids in the crowd directly. "What do snowmen eat, kids?"

Various answers float up. "Icicles!" "Water!" "Snowflakes!"

Raven shakes their head. "Snowballs!" And then their eyes take on a wicked gleam. "And what do they come out as?"

Nobody answers. People look at each other in amazement—is Raven really asking about snowman excrement?

Raven holds up a meringue and answers, "SNOW POO!" before popping one in their mouth.

You can hear a few people go, "Ew," but a ton of kids start chanting, "Snow poo! Snow poo!" and adults groan at the joke. I knew I shouldn't underestimate Raven.

When it's Marco's turn, he holds the tray up so the end of

the roll faces us, and we can see the pinwheel effect. It's pretty cool, I have to admit, but not super Christmassy. "Ube, purple yam, is a big thing in Filipino families—"

Filipino? One more thing I had no idea about. God, I suck.

"And my dad used to ask my mom to make an ube roll for every holiday, every birthday, every celebration, before he died." His dad is dead? Whoa. "Mom doesn't make it that often now because the memories still get her a little, but it wouldn't be Christmas without it. As long as he's been gone, he's with us for Christmas Eve when we eat his cake."

Huge applause. And no wonder—it's a touching story and a beautiful dessert made by a really cute, really nice guy. Raven shoots me a look, and I get it: he's safe for sure, so the battle comes down to us. May the second-best elf win.

I'm not sure what to make of the testing. One woman asks for my recipe, and I have to explain all the variations. The youngest judge, maybe eight, says it's good but "it doesn't taste *exactly* like peppermint bark."

Safety Mom, predictably, worries that the peppermint bits are a choking hazard. "I'd never let my children near these," she says while nonetheless finishing off a whole one herself. She tenders a tight smile. "But these are delicious." Do I get half her vote?

Out of the corner of my eye, I see a few people posing with their meringues for selfies, and I just know that #Snow-Poo will be all over Insta tonight. With so many people onstage, it's hard to see Marco at all, and while I'm looking, no-longer-a-mystery-judge Christa tries my whoopie pie. "Out-standing," she says, eyes sparkling. "Tell your dad he raised you right." Oh my god, his Christmas will be made.

The jingle of bells gets everyone's attention, and Victor holds the microphone. I hadn't expected the results so fast and hold my breath.

Instead, he promises to post our recipes online (um, I'll have to make one up . . .) and encourages everyone to come back tomorrow at noon, when the three of us become two of us, going head-to-head for the Top Elf prize. Not yet knowing who will make it is both a relief and a disappointment.

The rest of the day flies by—not gonna lie: I don't mind signing autographs and posing for selfies. I only had to clean up vomit once, and I never needed to bust out an Emergency Pop.

When I get to the command center, Victor is at his laptop, whistling holiday tunes. Today has been a big PR win for him, and I decide to use his good cheer to ask about Saturday. I clear my throat to get his attention, and he immediately hides his screen. "No results till tomorrow! You can wait!"

I see Marco, already changed into his street clothes, pretending not to listen a few feet away.

"No worries. I actually had a question about Saturday—"

"As long as that question is not about calling in sick or some other excuse, fire away!"

I freeze. How did he know? I think fast. "No, uh, I was just wondering if that's when the finale is. The pattern has been a challenge every other day, so . . ."

"*If* you make it, you get an extra day for this challenge because we want the big finish to be on Christmas Eve. It's going to be huge."

"Right . . . right . . . great," I stammer, and stumble away, no closer to asking than I was before. Victor's going to take more than a good mood to convince. Or maybe Dad will be the one to convince: he might have to have the party without me.

Marco waits till Victor is distracted and then corners me. "What's Saturday?"

"Shh," I say, no longer wanting to have this conversation with Victor today. I explain about the cookie party and how important it is to my dad. "Even *Christmas* comes second to Cookie Party. And his own *birthday* doesn't come within miles."

I'm expecting sympathy, but that's not what I get. "Then you should've said something!"

"What?"

His brown eyes reflect clear disappointment in me. "You can't throw in the towel like that!"

I take a step back. "You heard Victor. He's serious about this. I don't get to make the rules."

"If this means so much to your dad—and you're the guy who said 'I'm doing this for him'—fight a little harder. Tell Victor the truth. Make a deal or whatever—offer to work six hours instead of eight."

It doesn't matter if he's right. In fact, it makes it a little worse, because I know he is. But I don't love him telling me what I should or shouldn't do. What does he know about my life? I can't risk my chance at the money. With my grades, it's my only shot at replacing the scholarship. And if I don't go back, it'll help me and Dad while I figure out what comes next.

"I need this—"

"More than your dad? Family is all we have, right? In the end?" He doesn't say it, but I hear it clear as day: if his dad was alive, Marco would never choose a competition over him. It's a lot to put on me.

And then a thought comes into my head. It's petty and it's paranoid, but I can't shake it. "You're trying to get me fired! That's it. 'Cause you know you'll beat Raven." His lips part in surprise, before shutting into a hard line as I press on. "It's not like you need any help making the finals."

He folds his arms across his chest. "No," he says. "I don't."

Leroy comes out of a changing booth, looking really cute in an oversized mohair sweater in swirling colors that borders on ugly in that way really expensive clothes always do. He saunters over, eyeing my proximity to Marco. "Ready?"

Marco's eyes widen and then narrow almost immediately.

Oh shit. Leroy's assuming we'll head out together, which makes sense if he's my boyfriend again. Having promised Marco that ride, this is awkward.

"Uh, first, I have to—"

Marco shakes his head in disbelief. "No worries," he mutters. "I'm gonna go."

Seconds ago, I was mad at him. And now I feel terrible letting him walk away, but I have my pride too, so I don't call out. Why should I? I have a cute boy standing in front of me who isn't giving me crap about anything.

Leroy's eyes shine a little brighter, knowing he's won this round. "I'll swing by, like, nine? That okay?"

"Great," I reply, feeling anything but. I take his hand as we walk through the mall; something about a public display makes it feel true: we're a couple again.

When we get outside, though, snow is falling, and all I can think about is Marco biking home in it. Leroy kisses me again by my car, but my mind isn't in the moment. It's following a bicycle along dark country roads. I hope that Leroy can't tell.

The kitchen is empty when I get home, which is rare for Cookie Party week in general but more so with it only two days away. I find Dad in the living room watching an old episode of *Ted Lasso*. I join him on the couch and pull out my phone. "Look who it is," I say, thrusting the selfie of me and Christa Delcamp in his face.

He manages a tired smile. "That's great. Is she as nice in person as she is on TV?"

"Even nicer! And she said to tell you that you were raising me right." To my horror, Dad starts to cry.

Nobody likes to watch someone else cry, but it's doubly bad if it's a parent, because it's like, they're supposed to be the strong one, right? And it's triply bad when you know it's your fault.

"Dad, c'mon. It's okay. I didn't mean it yesterday. You know that."

He shakes his head, eyes closed but not stopping the tears. "No, I think you did. And it's fine—all the books say kids are supposed to separate from their parents at some point."

"Dad—"

"I just . . . I don't know. Maybe I did the wrong thing by going it alone all these years? I thought I'd find the right person, but I just threw myself so much into being a dad, I guess I let all that go too long. And now you have only me and it's not enough. I let you down."

"Oh my god! How can you say that?"

"You couldn't talk to me and there was no one else to talk to, and maybe if there had been, you'd be okay." He grabs tissues from a snowman Kleenex dispenser and blows his nose.

I scooch closer, trying to get him to look at me. "I *am* okay, Dad."

"Somehow everything caught up with me at once. I barely got through the factory today and called in sick to CVS. I guess this just kinda knocked the wind out of my sails."

"Is that why you're not baking? I'll help. We'll get your wind back."

He just shakes his head. "No need," he murmurs. "No need."

Patting my shoulder, he stands up and says he's calling it

a night, though it's only eight thirty, which is early even for him. But before he goes, he confesses that he can't bear the thought of everyone asking about my semester. "Every time someone asks, I'll be thinking, 'I should have known. I should have known.' I can't do that all night."

And then he says something he hasn't said in the eighteen years of my life. "I canceled Cookie Party."

He might as well have said Christmas is over. 'Cause that's what it feels like.

Eighth Day of Elfmas

Dad obviously doesn't want to be talked out of his decision because he leaves for work extra early, while I'm still in the shower. Though no Cookie Party will make it easier for me to win the Top Elf contest, the thought makes my stomach hurt.

Jazz has been texting since before I woke up. She is determined that we convince Dad to hold the party tomorrow after all. And nobody tells Jazz no. She announces that she is coming over to help me work on him tonight after my shift and makes me solemnly vow to reach out to friends to tell them to keep the time open.

I haven't exactly told her about my predicament. Maybe I won't. If the party does happen, I am just going to lie a little, tell her and my dad it's because I agreed to take an extra shift *after* he first canceled. Okay, maybe that's a little shitty of me, but it's less hurtful than the truth, right?

I play some Orishas, this Cuban hip-hop band my dad got me hooked on, while I choose an outfit. This morning I'm meeting Leroy at Buzz to make up for ditching him last night; after my dad's announcement, there was no chance I could go on a date. I don't own anything as nice as Leroy does, so I have to strategize: go classic (like a cable-knit sweater or turtleneck with a chain), or aim for something current, even if it's cheap? I riffle through my clothes, swiping back and forth through the rack, a magician turning cards, but never find a diamond.

Whatever. I don't want to be late—this is only my second time alone with Leroy since I've been back, and I want to make the most of it. I wore a sweater yesterday, so today I go with an oversized Burberry plaid vest over a mock turtleneck. Plaid passes the classic test, and the baggy vest is on trend, so hopefully it will do even though the Burberry in this case is knockoff from a sidewalk vendor in SoHo.

As I breeze through the kitchen, I see the purple food-dye bottle, and Marco's cake roll comes to mind. I picture him holding it up to show the crowd, that dimpled smile lighting up the stage. But then I see the look on his face when he realized I was making plans with Leroy. Ugh. I'll have to find a way to apologize later.

Buzz is busy when I arrive. As I walk in, Rena waves at me from behind the counter. I scan the room, but Leroy is not there yet. Bags has stolen my favorite booth, and seems to have really dug in today, with knitting supplies everywhere. I'm dying for coffee, but I decide to wait for Leroy to arrive, so I plop down in my second-favorite booth (the one where the tabletop is made of laminated tarot cards). I recognize a few kids back from college, and a few who should still be in class at high school. Earbuds is in his usual seat, jamming out to music no one can hear. Head bobbing atop a long, skinny neck, wispy hair catching little gusts of wind, he reminds me of an ostrich on parade.

I wait. And wait. And wait.

A prickling sensation, something like shame, starts to creep over me. I try to ignore it. Try to push the thought away as twenty minutes becomes a half hour and then forty minutes.

Finally a text arrives: Something came up. You understand.👻 Meet you at mall.

That's it? No apology, no heart emoji?

I read the message again: You understand.

This is retribution for me canceling last night. He sounded fine on the phone at the time, when, in fact, he was pissed. He's always had a tendency to nurse a wound and brood over any slight, so this isn't the biggest shock ever.

And I realize something: I'm not super eager to solve this problem. I didn't break up with him *just* because of college, but because I knew in my heart this wasn't a relationship worth trying to swing the long-distance thing. Getting back together with Leroy was like putting on your favorite summer-camp hoodie you've outgrown: it may be cozy and full of memories, but it's not a good look.

Honestly, the main thing Leroy offers me is a reminder of a time I didn't feel like such a screw-up. Driving to work, I think about how far away high school seems now. Drama club lead, class officer, National Honor Society, community service club, show choir—I mean, the yearbook is practically my personal photo album. I wasn't a disappointment then. That Cam would never have dreamed of this Cam: bad at school, single, neither a good son nor a good friend. Getting back together with Leroy now is less about him and more about *not failing* at something.

By the time I pull into the parking lot, I don't want to get out of the Fit. So I don't. I sit here and play "Winter Song" on repeat and stare at the cars filling the lot.

A rap at the window makes me jump. It's Marco. Ugh.

He motions for me to head inside the mall. I hesitate, but what am I going to do? I don't get paid for stewing.

The cold air blasts our faces as we head for the mall entrance. He acts like we didn't fight just last night, starts chatting away about this squirrel he saw trying to open a birdfeeder. I'm thinking that if my cheeks hurt this much from this short a walk, how must his feel after biking here? God, I'm a shit.

Before we go inside, I grab his arm. "I'm so sorry!"

He doesn't ask about what. His face takes on an additional glow. "Good!" He laughs. "'Cause I was so mad at you."

"Why aren't you now?"

He shrugs. "I hate being mad!" That's his answer? He opens the door. "I also hate being cold, so . . ."

"Tonight, I'm your ride home. No ifs, ands, or buts."

Marco heads inside, not looking at me as he asks, "What about Leroy? Seems like you two—"

I stop him again. (I'm touching him a lot. Interesting.) "We're really not an us." Marco raises an eyebrow skeptically.

"We were once, and I thought we might be again, but he may not be the nicest guy. . . ."

"Oh. So you like *nice* guys?" Marco nods approvingly, eyes gleaming.

"At least one," I say. And I look him right in the eye. For a moment, it feels like we're characters in a movie: shoppers pass around us on either side, but we're just standing there smiling at each other. I suddenly want to kiss him, and I can feel the changed air that says he wants to kiss me too, but it's kind of a strange place for a first kiss, and neither of us makes the first move.

Finally, he breaks the spell. "So far, I like today better than yesterday."

"And the fun has only begun!" I grab his hand and drag him to Biscuit Suprême.

The girl with the copper hair is not there, which is weirdly disappointing. I start explaining to Marco, "There's a redhead who works here who I like—"

"Kate? Yeah, she's great." Marco points out a specialty cookie at the back. "She hooked me up with a 'compost' cookie. There's potato chips in them."

"How do you know her?"

He looks puzzled. "From here. What do you mean?"

"I thought because you knew her name . . . Oh right: you're a 'people spy.'"

He laughs. "*Nice* guys do that. Ask the names of people they see every day. My mom loves cookies, and there's no Mrs. Fields in this mall, so I splurge and bring her one of these after my shift."

"You *are* nice." I groan. "I used to think I was. Now I'm wondering."

"It's okay. I'll give you lessons."

When it's our turn, I order a half dozen compost cookies and present them all to him. "Consider it a deposit on my tuition."

Raven, Marco, and I stand on the bandstand smiling and waving at the now too-big crowd. Santaland is way past its intended capacity, thanks to the megawatt charm of Christa Delcamp.

Her segment on 12 Days of Elfmas ran hourly during the morning news today, and it was a total valentine. Miranda says their whole family watched it before school, and Larry says his grandbabies just about set his phone on fire texting after. I had honestly forgotten all about it until arriving, so I had to watch the clip on my phone. I have to admit, she made us look good (and royal blue isn't such a bad color on me after all). Sadly for me, I also have to admit that if I was a home viewer, I'd vote for Marco.

Victor is at the microphone, tablet with the results in hand. Fiona has a big fake check at the ready, its face covered, while Larry and Miranda stand off to one side, Larry nodding encouragement to all of us, Miranda mouthing, "You got this," to Raven only.

If I don't make it, it solves the party problem, and I can be a good son and make Dad happy. If I do make it, I have a 50/50 shot of covering the second semester scholarship, which would make him happier in the long run. I don't know for sure if I even want to go back to NYU, but I do know I want the option. Please, universe, don't let Victor say my name.

"It's the moment you've all been waiting for!" Victor begins, and the crowd cheers like he's right. It's kind of amazing what people will get invested in. In November, nobody was thinking about mall elves, and yet here they are now, casting votes for us and following our elf pages and cheering us on. "Today, Top Elf comes down to just two. Who will we say goodbye to? Will it be Jingle? Raven? Or Oopsy?" Every name gets cheers and a few boos, though it's a little hard to tell whether people are booing us or the idea of us being eliminated.

Making a big show of reading his tablet, even though he knows the answer, Victor announces the results. "The elf who will not continue in the competition is . . ."

He's going to say Oopsy. I can feel it. My whole body tenses for the blow.

"RAVEN."

Raven's fans vocalize their love, and Raven comes forward, sporting an epic eye roll. I shoot Marco a look to say, *We did it*, but he shoots back a look that says, *It's* their *moment*, so I join the loud applause for them. Marco nods at me and heads toward Raven, and I do too. We go to embrace them from either side, but they flat-palm both of us to keep us away. The mic picks up them saying, "Not a hugger." The audience eats it up like it was a planned bit.

"I present to you our last two Top Elf finalists: Oopsy and Jingle!" Victor signals for the audience to applaud, but he needn't have bothered. They're noisy in their appreciation, and a singsong battle begins, some chanting "OOP-sy" and others replying "JIN-gle," like fans in an arena.

"OOP-sy!"

"JIN-gle!"

"OOP-sy!"

"JIN-gle!"

We pose for photos together, our arms around each other. Marco is waving to the crowd with one hand, while the other rests on the small of my back, a warm presence that feels so right. Someday, will we look at these pictures and think, *This was just the beginning*?

Victor quiets the crowd. "On Sunday the twenty-fourth, celebrate Christmas Eve right here in Santaland. You know Santa will have to fly back to the North Pole that night to get his sleigh ready, so we'll send him off with a song!"

Wait. Is he saying—

"The final competition will be Elf Idol. Oopsy and Jingle will be performing live on this stage—"

The crowd whoops at this idea, and I kind of do too: I have this in the bag. I may be majoring in experimental theater, but the musical-theater boy is always just below the surface. Plus, I mean, I've heard Marco sing. Enthusiastic and good are two different things, right? I don't dare look at him. Is he as disappointed as I am excited?

Victor sweetens the pot even more. "The rules are simple: both contestants will have to sing the same song. Any arrangement they like. But it has to be the same song, same tune, same words."

I steal a glance at Marco: to my surprise he's into it, nodding happily, unfazed by my obvious advantage.

"Everyone who votes gets ten percent off all sale items at participating retailers in the mall starting December twenty-sixth. Which is *also* the last day of Elfmas, the day when we name one of these guys Top Elf and he takes home the five-thousand-dollar cash prize."

He pauses. "Now I'm sure you're all wondering which song."

Um, *yes*. Will it be a classic, like "White Christmas"? Or something newer, maybe one of the Sia holiday songs? I'd kill for it to be "Wrapped in Red," but I don't think the universe favors me that much.

None of the above. "Well, it just so happens that we have a composer right here at Santaland!" We do?

Fiona joins him at the mic as he continues. "Our own Mrs. Claus, Fiona Shirleen O'Hara, has written an original number just for 12 Days of Elfmas—" Oh my god. *No*.

Taking the mic from Victor, Fiona addresses the crowd. "I just love the oldies but goodies—you know: 'Santa Baby' . . . 'Baby, It's Cold Outside.' Classics like these inspired me to write 'The Yule Log Song.'"

"The Yule Log Song"? Really?

She's in her glory. "I wanted something a little jazzy, a little swingy, even a little sexy." She winks on that line, seemingly forgetting she's still dressed in character. You can see the disconnect on parents' faces: Did Mrs. Claus really just say "a little *sexy*" and wink? Ew. Seeing their reactions, she hurries on. "I hope it becomes at least a *mall* classic! And it'll get its start right here on this stage in its world premiere Sunday—twice! So come see who sings it best!"

As the crowd applauds her exit, I'm still kind of reeling. I can only imagine what she has come up with. And I wouldn't say the visions are good.

I decide to use my half hour today to window-shop. I'm looking at a male mannequin in the window of Hugo Boss, working out how I can replicate the look cheaply, when I hear a familiar voice call my name. It's Ms. Kropp.

She's wearing a poncho, and her hair is pulled up today in a Ms. Frizzle pile, serving up nice auntie vibes. "I heard that Cookie Party is canceled. I hope everything's all right."

"Dad invited you? I didn't know." In all my life, he's never asked a teacher to come.

"Based on the guest list I saw, I think he invited a lot of people who are important to you."

Of course. It was supposed to be my triumphant return. I bite my lip, dying to just tell her the truth. The shame has not gone anywhere, but it would help to share it. "Um . . . I guess there's less to celebrate than there was. . . ."

When I have poured out my tale, Ms. Kropp leads me to a bench in the galleries and sits me down. "A lot of kids get to college and discover some things just aren't for them. If they're lucky, we're talking about nothing more than their major. But sometimes it's the whole school. And sometimes it's school, period. You're eighteen, Cameron—you have the time to mess up."

"Do I, though?" I explain that the scholarship was all that made it possible for me to be there. If I go back, there has to be some way to pay for it. "That's why I'm doing the whole Elf thing."

She waves that away. "You say that, but you're really doing this because you can't help yourself. You love to perform. Tell me you're not eating up the applause and the interview! One of my students even told me she got your autograph. Your *autograph*!" She pokes me in the arm, and I laugh. She's not wrong about me liking the attention.

"May I give you a piece of advice?" She doesn't bother pretending to wait for an answer. "Whatever this song is, find the humor in it. You have a knack for comedy; people are still talking about the wrapping paper."

"Except it's a singing contest—"

"And you'll dominate that piece of it. I know how good your voice is. But this is a *show*—give people what they want!"

Hmm. This seems worth considering, but I have to get back to Santaland before Victor fires me. I stand up and tell her how much I needed this visit. She hugs me in a way that feels like what people mean when they say "motherly." As she lets go, she makes a surprise offer.

"If you really don't go back to school, come work with me. I'm supposed to have a teacher's aide, but since COVID, nobody's applying. I've been doing it all myself all fall, so it would be nice."

This is so unexpected that I hug her again. Having another job lined up would be great, period, and working with her in theater, well, that would be amazing. But I'm confused. "So are you saying stay in school or drop out?"

"I'm saying *breathe* out." She chuckles. "This is a dilemma, not an apocalypse."

Even with the extra helpers, Santaland is a zoo today. There is just no keeping up with the volume. There are more criers, more kids needing quick escape routes to the bathroom, more vomit incidents—and stopping for photos and autographs doesn't keep the line moving. I'm paired with Kandy at Smooch Hollow, and I'm relieved to discover that she brings the same wacky intensity of her superfandom to being a helper. But every now and then I get the feeling she's shooting me, like, looks of love and adoration; I just make sure never to be beneath the mistletoe so that she does not seize her moment.

When it's time for my fifteen, I open "The Yule Log Song" sheet music Victor has sent to my email. I hate to admit it: it's not bad. I still don't know why they didn't go with a pop song—I mean, it's a *mall*—but I can work with this. Fiona has described it exactly right: it is a little jazzy, a little swingy, and a little sexy. The lyrics border on straight up suggestive, and I'm not sure it's super elf-appropriate.

Put another Yule log on the fire, baby
Rustle up some mistletoe
I've got a present you could unwrap, baby
Come on, Santa, let me elf you, ho ho ho . . .

Like, if Ariana Grande did it, it would be totally winky and amazing, but I'm singing to children. That's weird, right? The chorus doesn't let me off the hook.

Oh, the weather outside is frightful
But we find it so delightful
I think I'd like another night full
Of reindeer games with you know who
Merry Christmas to you!

Victor has sent an MP4 of Fiona singing the tune, and it's a trip. Her voice is nice, but she sings all husky like she's Eartha Kitt, and I feel awkward listening to my fifty-something boss crooning lines like:

Rudolph couldn't hold a candle to ya, baby
You could turn three kings to queens
Frosty woulda melted if he'd known ya, baby
Jingle bells, baby . . . you know what I mean

Wow. Beyond its heavy dependence on rhyming the word "baby" with itself, it makes me think Fiona isn't quite the wet blanket I'd imagined.

And then she's back on the chorus, riffing like she's Ella. Damn, though, it's catchy. I kinda wish I was singing it in a cabaret somewhere, but right now, trying it out in the break room, I'm not sure how it'll fly.

Marco shows up as I'm doing the chorus. He claps. "Well, at least one of us can make it sound good."

"You'll be great," I say, not sure he will. "We just have to hope nobody stones us."

We practice in the car on the ride home I promised, and it's nice. He's almost got the melody down, but he needs a lot of help doing the rhythm. Mostly, I lead—we don't listen to Fiona's recording more than we have to, because it's just too creepy to hear her singing "let me elf you." Honestly, we laugh as much as we sing. You could almost forget we're rivals.

As we roll into his neighborhood, he gets quiet. I don't know what's up. Is he thinking about the show or our fight last night?

He looks at me, serious. "I'm not trying to sabotage you, I swear, but . . . did you ask Victor about tomorrow?"

I keep my eyes on the road. We pass a house with a fully lit nativity scene, and the happy family seems to mock me. "My dad canceled the party."

"What? Oh no. It sounded great."

"It *is* great. I have to talk him out of it. My best friend is coming over tonight to try to help."

"How?"

"We'll just tell him how much it means to us both. To

everyone. Maybe we'll start baking—he hates to waste food, so if we're making more, maybe he'll just cave out of guilt?"

"And if you succeed . . ." He trails off. Good point. Then we're back to me getting out of work somehow. This week, every solution is a problem.

He reaches over and squeezes my leg comfortingly. And then he leaves his hand there. We're not embracing for a photo op; this touch is just for me, for *us*. It's quiet for a moment, and I turn to look at him; he's staring out the window, humming Fiona's tune to himself, and his face gets dappled, sometimes with Christmas lights as we pass houses, sometimes with only the moon. With his face at rest, the dimple almost, but not quite, goes away; you can still see how he's primed to smile. God, he's beautiful.

When we pull up to his house, his mom appears in the door. She's short and round-faced; the only commonality with Marco is the same beautiful skin and a pair of dimples that won't quit. I so want to kiss him right now, but I don't think I'm up for "Hi, I'm Cam and I'm going to suck face with your son for a minute."

Yet I don't want our time to be over.

He's lifting his bike out of the back and time is running out, when I blurt, "What are you doing tonight?"

"Practicing, I guess. I hear my competition's a good singer."

"Do you want to come over?"

The look in his eyes says *yes yes yes*, but he hesitates. "Won't that make it hard to talk to your dad?"

I laugh. "God no. It might even help. He'll be so happy I brought a boy home! That alone might be enough to get the party back on."

Marco looks at the door, where his mom gives a little wave. It's a moment before he looks back at me. "I want to . . . but I'm all Mom has. Knowing her, dinner's all cooked, so . . ."

"I get it," I say, disappointed, but understanding that he's right. "See you tomorrow."

"Call me *tonight*. I have to know how it goes." With his back to his mom, he blows me a kiss. It's corny-looking and stupidly sexy all at once. What has kept me from understanding before this that nice and hot are not mutually exclusive?

His mom opens the door, and he disappears into the realm of warm gold light beyond. When the door closes, taking the light with it, I just sit in the car a moment, looking at his house. It's simple, unspectacular, and yet it's magic, because I know that somewhere inside is the boy I'm falling in love with.

When I get to my place, Jazz is already there, and she and my dad are in the kitchen. I can smell something buttery baking, and my heart lifts. Has she done it already?

Dad gives me a hug the moment he sees me. "I'm so sorry. Jazz told me how sad you are about Cookie Party—she said you almost couldn't work you were so upset. And I felt terrible!" Behind him, Jazz is motioning for me to just go with it.

I play along. "You know, it's just . . . there are just so many memories and—"

He wraps me in a tighter hug, like an uncomfortable, you're-wrinkling-my-clothes hug. "I always thought the party was more *my* thing, but now I know what it means to you . . . Well, I'm calling everyone to say that it's back on!"

I untangle myself from my teary parent and hug Jazz instead. "Thank you," I whisper.

"No prob," she says, but I know she's proud of her skills, and that she will add this to her running mental list of things I owe her for. (The list is not small.)

Dad leaves us alone to work on a batch of the halva cookies that we always dye blue as a nod to Hanukkah. Jazz hands me the butter and sugar to cream, while my mind swirls. I'm psyched to see Dad so happy, but all I've really done is swap one problem for another. *Party's on—yay! Too bad I won't be there.*

I wait until Dad is talking to my tía Ely, a conversation that I know will be long, and whisper to Jazz. "I have a problem. . . ."

When I tell her that I don't actually have the day off work, she examines me like she is seeing a rare and bizarre species—*Ignoramus homosexualis*—for the first time. "Boy, you are a fool. You're letting him call everyone back to reinvite them to a party you won't be at!"

"I know!" I crack an egg into a bowl so viciously that shell pieces get in the yolk and I have to fish them out. "I *know.*" Mixing in the vanilla, I sigh. "On the way home, Marco said the same thing. He thinks I just need to tell Victor that I'm going to leave early for the party, but I can't."

Adding dye carefully to the mixed batter—too many drops would say blueberry not Hanukkah—she says, "*Marco?* What happened to Leroy?"

"No, Leroy is . . . Leroy is done. This is the other elf: Jingle."

Her eyes widen. "Damn, Cam! You and Jingle are going for rides now? Why did I not know this?"

"I . . ." I shrug. Even six months ago, I'd have texted her a blow-by-blow of this whole week, including the twists and turns of Marco and Leroy both. "I guess we got out of the habit. Like . . . once college started, you know, we haven't talked anywhere near as much."

She stops mixing the dough. "I tried," she says quietly. "But you took longer and longer to respond, so I just figured you were moving on." The hurt in her voice kills me. "I knew how badly you wanted to leave this town behind, and I thought maybe that included me."

I slump. I mean, I sort of knew that I wasn't being a great friend, and she's not wrong—I was focused on City Cam and his imaginary life. I fess up. "By the time I realized I was blowing it with you, I couldn't work up my nerve to call. I was worried you'd be mad at me. . . ."

"I was," she says. "You still should've called."

"I wanted to tell you how much I had messed things up, but I couldn't just be like, 'Sorry, I ignored you, and here are all my problems.'"

She shakes her head gently. "That is exactly what you should have done." She leans against me and gives me a nudge. "Note for next time."

"Note taken."

Dad comes back looking happy but a little glazed. "I lost a whole day of cookie prep. Why did I do that to myself? I'll be up all night!"

"We got you, Dad," Jazz says. "And I can come back early tomorrow, bring my girlfriend to help you set up, since this clown'll be at work."

"I forgot that!" Dad looks at me. "You won't be my prep boy this year! You'll just have to make it up to me by coming straight home in your costume. Think how fun it would be to have an elf here!"

"About that," I start, but Jazz glares at me. With best-friend telepathy, she makes it clear that I am *not* allowed to ask Dad if I can skip the party.

"Yes?" He's waiting for me to finish my thought.

"I might be a little late. . . ."

"Holiday traffic, I know. You just get here as fast as you can. We'll hold the carol till you make it."

Oh god, the carol sing. Each year Dad rewrites famous carols to include jokes about the past year's news and events. The first year of the pandemic had a "Twelve Days of Christmas" but with "seven sneezers sneezing" and "six swabbers swabbing"— that sort of thing. He prints out the lyrics, and everyone gathers by the tree to sing along, followed by a toast. The tradition has nothing to do with cookies, but it's the heart of the party. He always lets me set the key and lead the singing. Which will be pretty damn hard to do if I'm at the Reindeer Corral.

"Perfect," I say.

After Jazz leaves and the dishes are done, I crawl into bed, exhausted, and cuddle Kat Bizarro. Surprisingly, I get a text from Leroy. You up?

I think about this morning and I text back. No.

It sounds harsh, so I almost add "LOL" or some adorable sleepy face emoji, but then I don't. "No" is plenty.

Soon after, I get a text from Marco. Time to talk?

I don't hesitate.

YES 😊 😯 ♡

And now I'm not tired anymore.

Ninth Day of Elfmas

A good hot shower is my happy place. Strong water pressure and no one needing the bathroom is my idea of heaven. On a weekend, an hour-long indulgence isn't out of the question.

Naturally, it's a perfect concert venue.

Put another Yule log on the fire, baby. Rustle up some mistletoe . . .

Using the handheld showerhead as a mic, I practice the song over and over. I hate to give Fiona credit, but if there was a swing band or jazz combo in this shower, it really could be the stuff of Frank Sinatra. *I've got a present you could unwrap, baby . . .*

What it isn't, however, is *funny.* Or at least not ha-ha funny. Winky, sure; it's like the song version of suggestively raising your eyebrows. But it's not exactly comedy gold. If my fans (a phrase I never imagined saying when I entered the mall nine days ago) need me to make 'em laugh, as Ms. Kropp suggests, how am I gonna do that?

I try a funny elf voice. *Come on, Santa, let me elf you, ho ho ho.* Hell, that's even creepier.

Steam clouds fill the bathroom like a Turkish sauna. I change tactics and try the chorus straight, singing it like Justin Bieber doing R&B. *Oh, the weather outside is frightful, but we find it so delightful . . .* Nope.

Country? *I think I'd like another night full . . .* Uh-uh.

Hip-hop. *Of reindeer games with you, you, you know who! I said you know who!* God no.

Salsa? I do my best impression of my abuela Luci. *Mareee Creesmaaassss . . .* I do a few steps forward and back, shifting my weight from leg to leg. . . . *to you!* I make a big deal of a swivel and hip-check the shower caddy, which comes down in a torrent of shampoo, body wash, loofahs, and soaps; I slip and end up on the floor of the shower, laughing.

I can't wait to tell Marco.

Cookie Party is one of the few days of the year that Dad sleeps in. For him that means, like, seven, which wouldn't count for anyone else. But he allows himself that much time, then drinks a big cup of coffee and reads the newspaper on his phone. He says this is his calm before the storm, and it really is—he looks more relaxed than the other 364 days and 23 hours. As soon as his hour is up, he goes into host mode for the rest of the day: cleaning, cooking, arranging, greeting guests, refilling drinks and reloading cookie trays, and then cleaning every single bit of it up before he goes to bed, exhausted and happy as a clam. (Who decided clams were happy?)

When I come downstairs, he's still in his calm hour, cozy on the couch. He looks up. "Your friend called."

"Marco?"

He cocks his head. "Who's Marco?"

Oh, right—I told Jazz but not Dad. "He's one of the elves. And a potential boyfriend, maybe?"

Dad beams. "Not Leroy? You rascal! You have to tell me these things!" He motions at the phone in my hand. "Do you have a picture?"

"Oh—no, actually. It's kind of new. . . ." And then I remember. "It's on the app."

"What app?"

"You didn't download 12 Days of Elfmas? Really?"

He waves that remark away. "Social media is for you kids. I'll take real-life chat any day."

I start to explain that it's not social media, not exactly, but what's the use? Instead, I take his phone and download the app for him. I open it to the main page. I'd forgotten how silly my photo is, especially in contrast to Marco's, which is perfection. The app has the pictures posted side by side, with "JINGLE vs OOPSY," like we're prizefighters.

"Handsome!" Dad says. "Looks like a decent guy. I know you can't tell from a picture. . . ."

"In this case, pictures do not lie. He really is."

"Bring him to Cookie Party! Unless you're bringing Leroy."

"I am *not* bringing Leroy."

"Good!" He says this with an emphasis that makes me wonder if he had liked Leroy as well as I thought. "Can't wait to meet the new guy!"

Of course Dad wants him to come. How does he not understand that it's the second-to-last shopping day before Christmas and we work at a mall?

"No dice," I say. "He has to work. But . . . I hope you see a lot of him this Christmas."

As I head for the kitchen to get coffee, I realize we got off track. I poke my head back in. "So who called? And why'd they call the landline?" (Yes, we have one. Dad says I'll appreciate it when a solar flare or whatever kills cell service.)

"Your roommate again. Says she wants you to call her."

Seriously, I do not get this girl. It's no surprise she's up—Sarah Xu is too type A to waste her day sleeping. But why does she care if I go back? We're roommates, sure, but not *close*. I wasn't super nice to her or anything. Call her back or not?

I do, but from my room so Dad isn't hanging on my every word. Dialing her number feels strange because the call is ringing in a world that seems very far away from me right now. Not knowing what this call is going to be like, I instinctively reach under my bed for the Reese's Peanut Butter Cups. Who could blame me? I position Kat Bizarro on my lap so I have something to strangle if I need to.

"FINALLY," she says by way of greeting.

"Hey . . . You called?"

"And texted and emailed." (Who still reads email?) "And I only got this number because my girlfriend works in admissions and has no shame." Sarah Xu can't help herself; there is always an edge of fatigued disapproval in her voice, as if sometimes she tires of walking this earth with mere mortals. "I was afraid you weren't going to call me back."

I decide to be blunt. I mean, she's no frail flower. "I almost didn't. I don't get why you're bothering."

If you could hear someone purse their lips, it would sound like the ten seconds of silence that follow. And then she huffs, "Because, despite how clear it is that you think I'm some bossy know-it-all, I like you. I think you're funny and smart and talented. Everyone on our hall likes you. You just get in your own way."

"I what?" I can feel my face heating up.

"In class. You're *fire* in the dorm, but in school—you just don't show up. You worry so much about whether you're 'doing it right' and if we're taking you seriously that you're all defensive and guarded and shut down. Some lesser version of you comes to class, but who is that guy? The Cam who started the school year was gone by Thanksgiving, and this weird gloomy robot took his place!"

I can't speak. This is a lot. Is that how they see me? I gulp and try to find something to say. I gargle a weak rebuttal. "Maybe that guy knew he didn't belong in New York."

"You do!" The exasperation in her voice is profound. "Just not in ETW."

This lands in my chest. Not in ETW, the major I wanted so badly? The one that proves I am a serious actor?

She goes on. "You should be in musical theater. You should be singing and making people laugh—like you do in the dorm, but for real. Stop trying so hard to be the next Joaquin Phoenix and accept that you're a natural Hugh Jackman. That guy didn't win Tonys for being a brooding artiste; he won them by tapping into the human confetti cannon he was born to be!"

My eyes fall on the *Music Man* photo. Musical theater is the thing I left behind, part of outgrowing Lindell. But listening to Sarah Xu, I wonder why I decided it wasn't "real" acting. That I couldn't or *shouldn't* take it seriously.

"If you have a gift, one everyone can see, it's selfish not to use it! And selfishness is so irritating."

I think of Ms. Kropp's comment about my Hamlet making her miss my humor. I've been working so hard to tamp down the thing she loved about me, the thing my dad enjoys so much, the part of me that apparently my whole dorm could see me trying to run from. My head hurts as I wrap my mind around this.

"Thank you," I eke out.

"For saying you're irritating? Any time."

"I could have used this talk sooner, maybe. . . ."

She makes a derisive sound. "Because you and I talk so much, you mean?"

"Fair." I laugh. "But why now?"

"It never occurred to me that you would actually be so dumb as to leave instead of applying to switch programs."

"So why not let me?"

"Because it would be a waste and waste is as irritating as selfishness. *And* because I wrote you into my show."

Really? Sarah Xu?

She's explaining her concept, which I can't entirely follow, but it takes place somehow in cyberspace and there's tension between AI and scripted programs, and I'm a song sung live by a human, which messes with the scripted programs because it's, I don't know, original, and then the AI characters erase me so that the only voices are theirs? It sounds weird and maybe terrible, and I love her for wanting me in it.

"So?" she says. "Are you in?" I want to say yes, just to reward her for asking.

Maybe I am. Maybe I'm not. But I'll need to win that five thousand dollars to know for sure.

"What's this about a cookie party?" Victor's face has become an eggplant.

How the hell does he know about Cookie Party? My stomach hurts: Did Marco tell him?

Raven, Miranda, and Larry are at the table drinking hot cocoas, and they stop when they hear the tone of his voice. They look from me to him to me.

He answers the question I haven't asked. "I opened the app

just now, and imagine my surprise when your dad has used the Contact Us button to invite me to a party *today* as a surprise to you. Oh, and I can tell *all* the elves if I want! About this party *today*. He's so *sweet*, your dad—"

I have a Will Smith moment—get my dad's name out of your mouth, buddy—but I don't go pop him in the face.

"And he says to come as soon as we're done, anytime from four to eight. Four to eight today!"

"Okay, so—" I have to stop this train wreck.

"Which is funny because we're not done then. We're working until eight. Which he must know because that's why you told him you couldn't go to the party. YOU DID TELL HIM YOU CAN'T GO TO THE PARTY, RIGHT?"

Fiona, only half-Claused, steps out of one of the changing rooms. She looks at me, eyes wide. "Did you?"

Five thousand dollars is fluttering up, up, up, and away like a helium balloon in search of open skies. I will never touch that money.

Marco walks in, the bounce in his step seizing up once he sees the standoff at the O.K. Corral.

"I'm sorry. I just . . . I need to leave early, but I can work half the shift. It's just . . . this is my dad's biggest day of the year and—"

"AND you signed a contract." Victor turns to Fiona. "Fiona, did he sign a contract?" He doesn't wait. "He signed a contract." He marches up to me. "YOU signed a contract and you have been getting paid elf wages, not helper wages, because you did.

And that contract says you belong to me today. You belong to the parents and the kids. You belong to your fans! I did not work this hard making you an elf superstar to have you forget that."

Nobody moves. The vending machines hum. Strains of the mall Christmas playlist bleed into the room.

"What happens if I leave at four?"

"Then you're out. Don't come back. Forget the competition. Forget the bonus. And maybe don't cash your paycheck because I'm mad enough to sue you for breach of contract if you do."

This is an utter disaster.

"What if he doesn't leave?" Raven asks, not meeting my eyes. I think they're trying to buy me time, but it won't solve the problem.

Victor lowers his shoulders. "Then everybody wins. You all get to work. The kids are happy. The competition goes on. It will be the day you signed up for."

The air is heavy with expectation, and I can feel people willing me to stay. I don't know if I can. But I sure as hell can't decide with six pairs of eyes boring into my soul.

I throw up my hands in a gesture of surrender. It looks like assent, which is all Victor needs. It takes everything I have to control myself when he adds, "I'm sure the cookies will wait." Beneath the caterpillar on his lip, his smile is tight but victorious. "All right," he says, scanning the room. "Go make holiday magic."

★ ✳ ★

Because the universe hates me, Leroy is my helper in Santa's cottage. It's hard to field requests from parents when he keeps sidling up for whispered conversations. "Are you into me or not?"

I can't have this out here. Safety Mom and her two kids are next in line, so I make a big deal of greeting them. "Are you ready to see Santa? Make sure you know what you want to ask him for!"

Uncharacteristically, the little boy glowers at me. "Why? He's not gonna give it to us."

"Kumar!" his mother says, shocked. She looks like her last nerve has been worked. "I'm sorry. My children are not usually rude. I don't allow this behavior." I'm like, but maybe you model it?

I kneel by Kumar and his sister, asking her name. "Anjali," she says softly.

"Hello, Anjali and Kumar." I stick out my hand. "I'm Oopsy."

Anjali giggles. "I know."

"Sometimes our wishes don't come true very quickly, and sometimes they're in disguise—we think we are wishing for one thing, but what we really want is something else, and we don't know it till we see it, and then we finally know what we were really wishing for all along."

Kumar puzzles this out. "Huh?"

"I just mean make your wish anyway. Tell Santa. And maybe

it won't come true this Christmas, but it'll be out there. And someday it will come back to you."

Kumar and Anjali whisper to each other, and then he looks at me, nodding solemnly. "Okay."

When I stand, Safety Mom is looking at me differently. She squeezes my hands. I can see her wrestling with what to say. Finally, she settles on something. "I hope you win."

When the kids are settled in for the photo, both whisper to Santa at once, and I am 100 percent sure they ask for a house.

A house?

I can't see Safety Mom's eyes because she is focused on watching her children. But the spoiled-rich-lady narrative I made up for her is unraveling in my head. How does a woman with a Coach bag and such entitlement not have a house? Scenarios fly through my head—maybe her spouse died and they ran out of money? Or maybe her partner took up with someone else and locked them out? Maybe she was a single mom all along and their house burned down? I have no way of knowing, but suddenly I'm open to the idea that she might be difficult because of stress and that she may be here every single day because they are houseless, and wherever they are staying at the moment, it isn't a place they want to be.

Leroy is ushering them out, and I'm trying to whip up cheer for the next family, but I keep thinking about those two words: "A house." Things are always a little tight for Dad and me, but I've never worried we'd lose our home, which he is scenting with cardamom rolls right now—and which will be full to the brim but one son too empty if I stay here till eight.

I jump when Leroy reappears, whispering, "If we're gonna get back together, you need to act like you want it."

This is supposed to be kind of a threat, but I hear something else underneath: surprise that I'm not chasing him.

"Got it," I snap back.

He frowns. "Yeah?"

"The rules are clear: Ask you to take me back and you will. And if I don't, you won't."

"Close enough. . . . So which is it?" We're not even pretending to move the line along, and parents are grumbling. Maybe about waiting, maybe about being forced into witnessing elfin divorce court.

I take a step back and cross my arms, fixing him with a look of sheer disdain. "Does it look like I'm asking?"

His jaw drops and his eyes widen before his face becomes a mask. "Wow," he says. "I knew I could do better."

Finally doing his job, he leads the next family forward. I pull candy canes from my tunic and press into the crowd, apologizing for the slowdown. I have work to do.

At 4 p.m., I return to the command center to tell Victor I have made my decision—which is to go home. I'll return my costume and grab my bag, and that will be that.

When I get there, it's empty save for Victor himself, which is a little sad, since I won't get to say goodbye to anyone, but also a relief, since I'm guessing this won't be pretty.

"Thank you for the opportunity—" I start.

"Which you're blowing!" he retorts. "And now I'll have to do cleanup!"

"I'm sorry."

"Sure, sure," he says, snatching off my elf cap and making a gimme motion so that I turn over my stash of candy canes. Then he motions me toward the back wall, where a drop cloth covers some unseen object. With a bullfighter's flair, he pulls away the fabric, revealing giant standees of me and Marco in our elfwear. "Do you know how hard it is to turn around standees in twenty-four hours? These cost a fortune! And tomorrow is Sunday! If I wanted to get one of Raven to replace you, I couldn't do it!"

"Um, okay . . ."

"AND THE INTRO VIDEOS!" He sounds like he's close to an aneurysm. "I know the guy who does the contestant videos on *America's Got Talent*, and even with a discount, they weren't cheap. YOU'RE COSTING ME MONEY!"

"Not if you let him compete." Marco has appeared as if from nowhere. *Of course* he came, but beaming in like that startles both me and Victor into silence. He repeats himself. "You make the most money if the contest goes on the way it's supposed to."

"We both know that won't happen." Victor's sneer is profound.

"Do we?" Marco says, walking toward Victor, looking very, very calm and very, very determined.

"What is that supposed to mean?" Victor's surety is less strong than just a moment before.

"It means that Oopsy and Jingle have brought Santaland so many followers that it's twice, three times, as busy as before the competition started, so we're making you money. And you'll make more tomorrow if there's a big turnout for the sing-off, which will be *way* less likely if Oopsy and Jingle *both* quit because their boss wouldn't give them four hours off."

"Both?" Victor gasps.

"Yeah, I'm going to the party too."

I could kiss him so hard right now.

Victor stands stock-still. Calculating. You can see him running through his options: if he fires me, he can replace me with Raven, a popular choice, even if it means no standee, no fancy video. Replacing us both is harder—who gets the other spot? Larry and Miranda were both cut at the same time. Does it even matter? If it's Raven versus either of them, the outcome will be a foregone conclusion. All the suspense will drain from the competition the way the color drains from his defeated face now.

He waves dismissively. "Do what you want. Tech for the sing-off is at eleven." He pretends to find something on his tablet very interesting as we both head for changing booths. I'm inside, heart pumping with adrenaline, stripping off my tunic, when he adds a last thought: "But no bonus for the loser!"

★ ✳ ★

The drive to my house is a rush. We practically ran through the mall after I changed into my new Zara shirt, and now we're flying down the roads of Lindell like we're trying to get a DeLorean up to speed for time travel. I start off playing "Butter" by BTS—a litmus test of whether we have a future—and I'm psyched to discover that he knows all the words. But it's not long before we ditch BTS for our competition song.

Rudolph couldn't hold a candle to ya, baby! You could turn three kings to queens!

We're belting Fiona's song for all we're worth, even if it would be wiser to save our voices for tomorrow. On *Frosty woulda melted if he'd known ya, baby*, Marco goes floppy, sliding half out of his seat, and I'm dying with laughter.

My house isn't very big, and the driveway is proportionately small; it can fit two cars at best. Today, somehow three are squeezed in dangerously, and cars line the road for a solid block on both sides. In the past, Dad has invited as many as sixty people to Cookie Party, which is a lot for nine hundred square feet, but I'm thinking he's blown by that number now.

We park up the street on the shoulder, and I turn off the car. "Are you ready?"

"Am I ready?" He grins. "I risked five thousand dollars for it, so . . . these cookies better be amazing."

We snake our way between the cars in my driveway, and just before I open the door, he takes my hand in his. It makes me so happy, I could burst, but he sounds shy when he asks, "So, are we . . . like . . . ?"

"A couple?"

"Would you like to be? I would."

I'm so happy he asked I can't even speak. I just lean in for a kiss, but I'm thwarted when Dad flings open the door and throws his arms around me.

"Cam-Cam!" He releases me and turns to Marco. "And you must be—"

"My *boyfriend*, Marco," I say, answering two questions at once. I swear they're both so happy it's almost hilarious.

The carol sing is wrapping up. Dad has already gotten through "Climate Change Is Coming to Town" and "Away with a Stranger," about this cult kidnapping everyone was talking about all summer; his big finish is a "Hallelujah" chorus that replaces the word "Hallelujah" with "Dolly Parton" because she is like his patron saint (and maybe the only deity I sign off on). Marco has his arm around me, and it feels like it was built just for this.

Ms. Kropp shoots me a look from across the room, nodding as she sings along. I smile back, grateful that she can see me happy instead of just moping. When the carol ends, she is the loudest in cheering Dad on. He blushes and raises his hands to calm everyone. Reaching for a glass of his famous bourbon punch, he clears his throat.

"I'm so glad you could all be here tonight to celebrate Christmas and to celebrate Cam being home. It's great to see friends, both old"—he toasts Jazz, who blows him a kiss—"and new," he says, steering all eyes toward Marco. Marco doesn't shy from it; he takes a little bow and then gives me a peck on the cheek. (The cheek? This so does not count as our first kiss.) "We never know what's coming"—I'm pretty sure that part's just for me—"but though we can't see ahead, I still know the future is merry and bright! Salud!"

A chorus of "saluds" and cheers follows, dispersing the crowd back into little clusters of people who know each other holding court in their usual spots, guests who are new trying to make friends at the cookie table, and my relatives in the kitchen. Ely and Mari practically drag me and Marco to the island. Mari is all business. "Where are you from? What do your parents do? Are you in college?"

Ely slaps her arm. "Sister. Let them be." She winks at Marco. "We'll give you the third degree tomorrow."

"What's tomorrow?"

"We all go to Mar's for Noche Buena—it's a Christmas Eve thing."

"I know! Mom's from the Philippines; we do it too. But . . ." And he trails off.

Mari is great at homing in on the unspoken. "Are you not doing it this time? How come?"

He hesitates. "It's no big deal. It's . . . it's just been a long year."

Ely claps her hands. "That settles it. Bring your mom. We roast a whole pig—the difference between fifteen people and seventeen is nothing."

While Mari keeps up the questions, I wonder. Did his dad die that recently? He's so cheerful all the time that it's almost easy to forget that he's a real person. And that real life is never as perfect as it seems.

Jazz and Annika join us at the island. "Did you see her kransekake?" Jazz asks.

"One, I do not know what a kransekake is. And two, we still haven't made it to the cookie table!" Suddenly I'm so hungry I could eat every single thing in the house.

Jazz parts the crowd so we can see the kransekake, a tree made of stacked almond cookie rings that get smaller and smaller as they rise. It is drizzled with white icing and studded with little Norwegian flags. The top few rings are gone, but it's still an impressive sight.

"You *made* this?" Marco exclaims and fist-bumps Annika. "I'm so jealous."

Annika starts explaining how it works and he listens closely, as Jazz leans in and says, "Why weren't you with this one all along?"

I just laugh. "Would you believe it was because he seemed too nice?"

She rolls her eyes. "From you? Yes, I would. Fool."

The kransekake may be the star, but it's hardly alone. There's just so much, the plates overlap. Christmas wreaths, gingerbread, raspberry thumbprints, lemon bars, seven-layer headache bars, three kinds of fudge, brownies, blondies, choco-late cookies in three different sizes, cranberry oatmeal cookies, shortbread, World Peace cookies, macaroons *and* macarons, blue halva squares, rugelach, peanut butter buckeyes, popcorn balls, and Jazz's specialty: homemade Pop-Tarts. This spread is a deadly sin.

When we've filled our plates, I nod for them to follow me out back.

It's too cold to sit out here without our coats, but the sky is so clear and bright with stars that we tough it out. The four of us talk and laugh so easily, it's like we've always been a quartet. I can hear the music playing and see my dad talking to Ms. Kropp through the window, and I think maybe for the first time in a week, I feel my shoulders relax.

"Where do you go to school?" Annika asks Marco, as innocent a question as can be at our age.

"Oh . . . um . . ." Marco's face is shadowed, so I can't see what's going on. "I was going to go to Wachusett, but, uh . . . I'm just doing some online courses now." There's clearly more to this, and he can see we're hoping he'll explain. He tells the whole story, most of which I haven't heard. His dad had a great job at Pioneer Valley Medical, but he also had a heart condition that wasn't supposed to be a problem till he was an old man. He'd never expected to drop dead at forty-five, when Marco was seventeen; the year since, while his mom looked for work, has eaten up most of the savings they had.

"When my folks were first married, Mom was a travel agent, but she gave it up to stay home with me when I was little—always said it was a blessing." By the time she needed to go back to work, her old career pretty much no longer existed, and she couldn't find much else, so she became a housekeeper. In a painfully short window of time, she went from stay-at-home mom with a middle-class life to cleaning the houses of her dead husband's coworkers. "Women she went to holiday parties with last Christmas are now her bosses."

Whoa.

"The money isn't actually horrible because she's so good at it, and there are always clients. But there are no contracts—people can stop whenever or just skip a few weeks—which means things are a little unpredictable." And, of course, he adds, there are no health benefits. "When she was diagnosed with diabetes, the insulin was off the charts, and they were like, 'You're just going to have to find a way to pay.'"

He is quiet for a minute. No one is eating cookies now. "She's still working, and I got a job at a bike shop to help. I just do a class at a time for now. . . ."

Jazz cuts in. "But that'll take forever."

"I know," he murmurs, and looks up at the stars. "But until the universe decides to give us a break, I'll make the best of it." He holds up his cookie plate, deploying that smile I love. "And this is a pretty good start. In less than an hour, I gained a boyfriend, two new friends, and all these cookies. Not bad."

Jazz takes both my shoulders in hand. "This guy, Cam? This guy is a keeper. Do. Not. Blow. It."

Annika stands, rubbing her arms. "It's too cold out here. I'm going inside. Come on, Smoosh," she says, motioning for Jazz to follow.

"SMOOSH?" I can't believe I heard that right.

"Say a word and you're dead to me." Jazz laughs, following Annika.

"That was nice of her," Marco says when we're alone.

"What?"

"The Norwegian pretending it's too cold—pretty sure she just knew how much I wanted to be alone with you."

And this is it. There is always that moment before a kiss when you just know. The air shifts, as if electricity is rearranging the particles, and expectation becomes a kinetic thing. He pulls me close, and his lips find mine. It's gentle at first, a hello. He pulls on my lips with his teeth, then parts them with his tongue. I taste him, and then he is tasting me. My hands go to his hair, while his encircle me. We kiss and kiss and kiss. It's not quiet, not subtle. You can probably hear us at the neighbors', we're so into it. And when we finally stop, we're both breathless.

"What was that?" I say, gasping.

"*That*," he says, "is what I've been dreaming about all week."

When we head inside, I'm pretty sure I have clown mouth, which is what Jazz calls it when you kiss someone so long and so much that your lips are swollen and there's a red glow around them. She spots my condition immediately and gives me a thumbs-up. I'm waiting for Dad to notice, but I don't see him anywhere.

Annika, who seems to have decided Marco is her new favorite person, hustles him into the living room, where my tías have pulled out my dad's photo albums and are telling stories about me. I skip this particular thrill and head into the kitchen instead.

My dad and Ms. Kropp are alone at the island, where he is explaining to her the history of his prized holiday decoration: the Snowmama. When I was fourteen or fifteen, someone at Dad's church arranged a group to book a Russian river cruise. The highlight of the trip was a matryoshka doll market. He had always been fascinated by nesting dolls, the ones with six or eight of the same doll in successively smaller sizes, each hidden within the doll before. It felt like providence when he found a set in St. Petersburg that looked like a roly-poly snowman but wearing a Russian head scarf, like a babushka. He dubbed it the Snowmama and bought it on sight, without even opening the set. He was back on the boat before he realized just how special it was: there were actually *twenty* Snowmamas inside, the tiniest one the size of a thimble.

He keeps Snowmama on its own shelf in a hutch, and it was the one snowman I couldn't play with as a child. He never brings it out at Cookie Party because he's afraid he'll lose a piece. Yet here is Ms. Kropp, holding the two smallest Snowmamas in her hands, making them whisper to each other in fake Russian. My dad has his hand on his chest, laughing.

It's well after eight, and most folks have left by this point. I start picking up some of the plates and napkins. The doorbell rings, and I can't imagine who it would be. Of all the options that come to mind, Raven and Miranda did not make the list. Yet here they are. Out of elfwear and standing side by side, they seem more clearly siblings to me now: both have narrow, inquisitive faces, and I never before noticed how similar their eyes are. "You guys came!"

"I don't see any 'guys,' but yes, we did," Raven says. "Marco texted. Said we could still have cookies."

Miranda looks pained. "I told Raven we should stop to pick some up, that it's rude to show up empty-handed, but nothing was open on the way."

"Oh, it's okay," I say, laughing. "We're not short on cookies." I lead the siblings to a now-chaotic table that looks like a cookie cannon has been firing treats at it randomly. "We always have tons left over, and we donate a bunch every year. So eat up!"

Raven needs no encouragement at all, filling a plate in about five seconds, and then barrels into the living room, asking, "Where are these embarrassing photos you texted about?"

Miranda takes my arm. "Larry says hi. He had to get home before his wife 'skinned him alive' as he put it. But he wants you to know he loves what you two did." She lowers her voice though we're alone. "I don't think he likes Victor very much."

"Do you?" I ask.

She wrinkles her nose. "I think he must be kind of unhappy to be this wound up all the time. I pray for him."

"Do you pray for me?" It just kind of pops out. I never imagined anyone praying for me, but I'm shallow enough that I don't want to be left out if she is.

"Mm-hmm." She nods. "And Larry and Fiona and Marco. It's just who I am."

I'm surprised how sweet this feels; it may not be *my* love language, but it's hers. I don't ask what her prayers entail, and instead, I tease a little. "Did you pray that Raven would beat me?"

She trills a laugh. "Twice a day. At least!"

From the living room, we hear Raven. "You have to see this, Randy." A nickname they have never used for their sister at work. And she darts off to join them.

I stand in the doorway and look in. Marco has a tía on either side of him, with Jazz and Annika sitting on the arms of the couch, as all five work their way through what I'm pretty sure is my eighth-grade yearbook. But now Raven and Miranda—*Randy!*—sit on the floor, craning to see. I should be mortified: eighth grade was the year before I discovered the power of Clearasil. But how can I not love this? They look like a big family at story time.

Quietly, I snap a photo on my phone. This is a picture I never imagined, and I want to keep it forever.

Tenth Day of Elfmas

It's too early for Reese's, right? Morning light reaches into my room but not all the way to my Playbills, which means it's not even eight yet. Sunday morning and I'm eighteen, which should equal sleeping in, but I'm awake and I have been for a while.

What am I doing?

Sarah Xu's call has me seeing NYU through new eyes. Maybe I could have a place there after all, if I'm willing to swallow my pride and switch programs. I see myself in the ensemble of a musical, sweating my way through bows at a noisy curtain call. I can almost feel the electric thrill of a cheering audience again. . . .

But what if I still don't fit in? What if I never find my people? Will I have wasted Dad's hard work on a dream I shouldn't have chased? I know he wouldn't like to hear me put it that way. He's already said he'll find a way to cover the lost scholarship no matter what, if it means I'll give it another shot. But I know how hard that will be on him.

The safer, more responsible bet is to stay. I could take Ms. Kropp up on her offer. It could give me space to figure out what's next *and* help Dad out. I know he'd kill for more time with me. So would Marco.

Marco. Just thinking of him floods me with warmth. I've never known anyone quite like him—a heart so good it makes him beautiful. In comparison, it's hard to believe I ever found Leroy so appealing. If I stay and Marco is only in school online, we could really have something. I imagine our first New Year's (yes, silly hats, which *he* won't say no to) and Valentine's (I'll learn some Filipino dessert to surprise him) and—

Wait. What am I doing?

Do I want to stay here for a boy? I know what I'd say if it was anyone else. Ugh. What if me staying ends up being a new way to fail us both? Forget what time it is; I pop a peanut butter cup in my mouth.

And no matter which choice I make, the five thousand dollars looms over my head. If I win, I can afford to go back to NYU with less guilt about Dad. But I'll always know what that money could have meant for Marco. Here I am wanting to make it *easier* to pay for college, when he can barely afford even one class at a time. If I win, he loses more than just a competition. That settles it.

I sit up, suddenly sure of my plan.

It's so clear to me: I need to throw the competition. I can't cost Marco such a big opportunity. It can't look too obvious, because he's got his pride. I'll just have an Oopsy fail and pretend to be a good sport when he takes home the prize.

Visions of NYU start to fade, and I tell myself it's fine. I'm not dropping out because I like Marco but because *I* can be a good guy too. I'll stay home, work hard, and have a great semester with my new boyfriend. His life will be easier, so will Dad's, and I'll never again have to worry about City Cam. Maybe Lindell Cam is where it's at after all.

Feeling lighter, I put the near-empty bag of peanut butter cups away. I don't need them anymore.

Turns out that Victor has hired a swing band to back us up. They're all my dad's age, and they're super enthusiastic, maybe more than the song deserves. Marco is nowhere in sight, so I can practice alone. Well, not quite alone; Fiona is on the floor below the bandstand, watching me with a look akin to horror. I'm not taking the first line of the chorus at the tempo she wants, and it obviously pains her.

She models how she envisioned it, and I try it again, which gets a nod of approval. But then I let her down on the next line. She wants me to warble like I'm riffing on a saxophone. Fine, I do it her way.

It's like this all the way through until the song sounds like she imagined. I can't find a way to make it bad enough to lose with her so close, so I give up and do it right. The band starts to get into it, and Fiona's eyes gleam. "Perfect!" she calls out.

"Perfect!" I'm pretty sure it's the first time all week she has praised me for anything.

When I come down off the stage, I return the favor. "You should be a music teacher—you're good at it."

A shadow crosses her face. "I was. For twenty-five years. Until they cut my program and expanded football. But thanks." She heads up onstage to confer with the band, and I am chastened. *Everyone* has a story.

I wait by the bandstand till it is almost noon, and Marco has not taken the stage. Maybe he practiced at home? Or maybe I missed something and he got here before me. Either way, I have to get dressed for the show.

In the changing room, I have my elf tights on but not my tunic, when Marco, in full Jingle attire, pulls back the curtain, steps in to join me, and slides the curtain shut again. He motions for me to be quiet.

Don't get me wrong: it's heaven to be so close to him, but it's also weird. "What are we doing?" I whisper.

"I'm going to throw the song," he whispers back.

"What? You can't do that—*I'm* going to!"

He looks surprised. "But you need it for school!"

"Me? You need it for everything!"

He shakes his head. "This money won't get me into college this year. At least *one* of us should be on track. Let me do this."

"No," I say, "I'm not letting you. No chance."

Marco pouts (which is, no surprise, a cute look on him). "What if I go first? I'll just blow it before you can stop me."

"The power of going last means no matter how bad you do, I'll do it worse. I'll make your fail look like a win."

"What if I don't sing at all?"

"Then I won't either, but I'll also flip off the crowd and swear at Victor from the stage!"

He groans. "You're killing me!"

"No," I say, "I'm kissing you." And I plant a big fat one on his lips. He kisses me back and then folds me into his arms. I rest my head on his shoulder and sigh, content, despite the ridiculous context.

We hear Fiona and Victor enter the command center. We both freeze and hold our breath. We know exactly what it would look like if they discovered us all tangled up in this dressing room. Victor speaks, but I catch only the end of what he's saying. ". . . and that little solidarity stunt they pulled yesterday."

Fiona agrees. "It's like they don't know they're competitors!"

"You wouldn't think I'd have to write 'no office romance' into the contract."

"Raven was right?" She sounds genuinely surprised.

Victor snorts. "Isn't it obvious? Marco's been mooning over Cam all week, and Cam finally caught up. Anyone with eyes can see it!"

Fiona harrumphs. "Well, I didn't, and *I have eyes!*" She says this like it's a point of pride. Marco starts to giggle at this, and I clamp my hand over his mouth as she goes on. "If they had any sense, they'd channel that into the contest. It's a love song, after all."

"How do I get it through to you: I don't *want* lovebirds—it's a *battle*! I want *fighters* going head-to-head. Nicki and Cardi, not Romeo and Romeo!"

We hear footsteps and there's a third voice, which I recognize as Kandy. "Prancer won't turn on. He's stuck in the head-down position."

"It never ends!" Victor cries, and we hear all three leave the room.

We burst out of the booth, laughing with nervous relief. "Can you imagine if they caught us?" I ask, breathless.

"They still could." He grins. "Put your clothes on, Romeo!"

I'm buttoning up my tunic, thinking about what Victor said. "We're that obvious, huh?"

Marco does a spot-on imitation. "Anyone with eyes can see it. . . ."

Boom. Inspiration strikes. "You know who has eyes?" I ask. "The *audience*."

"Okay . . ." Marco waits for more.

"I know just what they need to see."

Combine the last shopping day before Christmas with all the social media hype around 12 Days of Elfmas and the crowd is huge. Not only is Santaland full, but the galleries are lined with shoppers who have paused to watch.

Victor isn't letting go of this battle royale idea. He's having us enter to the theme song from *Rocky*, some boxing movie I've never seen, and he wants us to jog in like prizefighters. Marco is a good sport, pumping his fists in the air as he pads toward the bandstand, voices calling his elf name and whistling.

There is not even the slightest part of me that wants to fake being a boxer, so when it's my turn, I go full Oopsy instead, pretending to be lost and letting the crowd steer me toward the stage. People are laughing (Ms. Kropp would be proud), and chants of "Oopsy" echo across the atrium. I dig it.

"It's the moment of truth, 12 Days of Elfmas fans. The final battle. The showdown. The rumble in the jungle. The thrilla in Manila." I have no idea what he's talking about, but I'm onstage, so I nod and smile, nod and smile. "It all comes down to this: after both elves sing the new holiday classic 'The Yule Log Song,' then *Yule* decide who did it best!" Oh my god, he's so proud of that pun he's actually glowing.

"Jingle will perform first, followed by Oopsy. You can vote online and on the app through midnight on Christmas, and we'll see you back here on the twenty-sixth as we crown a win-ner *and* the Shops at Vision Landing kick off their Great Final Sale, up to fifty percent off mall-wide—on top of your ten per-cent off for voting!" (It's the wrong moment to think of this, but 60 percent sounds really good. . . .) "For now, settle in for the main event. Call it Pioneer Valley Idol. Call it Vision's Got Talent. Call it the Elf Factor—it's time for the Top Elf Sing-Off!"

Victor leads me off the bandstand so that Marco has the stage alone. The drummer starts a rhythm on the snare, and then the piano joins, sounding the melody of the chorus.

Marco's smile has a bit of a nervous edge, and he grabs the microphone stand as if holding on for dear life.

He's only sung the first line—*Put another Yule log on the fire, baby*—when I bolt for the stage and swagger up to the mic, grabbing it out of his hands. "Imma let you finish," I say. "But I have one of the best versions of this song of all time!"

The crowd roars, some getting that I'm spoofing the famous Kanye West–Taylor Swift meme, and some just loving the obviously fake drama. Marco grabs the mic back. "Oh yeah? Mine is way better." (Okay, he isn't a super-convincing actor, but I'm the one in theater school and he's not, so . . .)

Victor is motioning for me to leave the stage, his face bulbous with fury. "GET DOWN!" he whisper-shouts, but I stay put. Marco motions for the band to take it from the top.

I start, hamming up the cheesy romance of the lines.

Put another Yule log on the fire, baby
Rustle up some mistletoe

Marco undoes the top button of his tunic, eliciting whistles and screams as he takes the next two lines:

I've got a present you could unwrap, baby
Come on, Santa, let me elf you, ho ho ho . . .

And then we're singing together.

Oh, the weather outside is frightful
But we find it so delightful
I think I'd like another night full
Of reindeer games with you know who
Merry Christmas to you!

He leads the next round:

Rudolph couldn't hold a candle to ya, baby

You could turn three kings to queens

Naturally, I sashay and shantay like I'm on *RuPaul's Drag Race.*

When I sing, *Frosty woulda melted if he'd known ya, baby*, he goes floppy like he did in the car.

Jingle bells, baby . . . you know what I mean

I check out how Victor is doing. He is pretending to be into it, bouncing, nodding, like he's just any other fan, but his face is an absolute stone.

From the bandstand, I see a lot of familiar faces in the crowd. The red-haired biscuit girl is taking pictures from the galleries. Jazz and Annika have somehow managed to get into the Santaland line without kids and are bopping to the song. Leroy stands by the corral, arms crossed, face stony. A few feet away, Kandy is filming with an earnestness that suggests this will go into her permanent archive. Safety Mom is listening with her eyes closed, and she almost seems at peace.

I'm already thinking ahead to the big finish. Before we came on, I taught Marco a quick spin-and-return move for the last bit. He basically has to stand in place and let me do the work. Hopefully I won't Oopsy.

Oh, the weather outside is frightful . . .

He spins me away.

But we find it so delightful . . .

He spins me back, so we are side by side.

I think I'd like another night full

He turns me to face him.

Of reindeer games with you know who . . .

He lifts me up like it's *Dirty Dancing*, the crowd losing its collective mind.

And just like that we're at the final *Merry Christmas . . . to you*. It's over, not a single flub. We've done it.

The once-quiet farm fields upon which this mall was built have never in millennia heard noise like that which fills the atrium now. You'd think it couldn't possibly get louder, but trust me, when Marco surprises me with a kiss, right there in front of everyone, it does. In Florida, they can't even *say* gay to kids, but here in Massachusetts, we act it out.

This should be where the story ends, right? Total triumph. Gay icons and local heroes, we split the prize money. Literal win-win.

But Victor isn't having it. Returning to the stage, he pretends to be pleased. "What a show, right?" The crowds whoop it up. "I've never seen opponents play quite that nice before . . . which will make it all the harder when you vote!" He pretends to read from his tablet; from behind him, only Marco and I can see the screen is dark. What is he up to?

"I'd sure love to reward both these guys, wouldn't you?" Applause confirms this. "But the rules *clearly* stipulate that only one winner can take home the prize. By law, I'm not allowed to split it." By law? *Come on.* "I feel as bad as you do, but my hands are tied." A few boos filter down from the galleries. Murmuring takes over. The crowd does *not* love this turn.

From the side, I can see that Victor is enjoying this power. "The good news is that they're each other's biggest fans. I take great personal comfort in knowing that the loser will cheer on the winner just as much as you and I. So don't forget to vote. Let's make one of these elves FIVE THOUSAND DOLLARS richer!" Saying that number is enough for him to win the crowd back over, and he stokes their enthusiasm. "Who will it be: Jingle?" This merits rowdy cheers. "Or Oopsy?" My fans make themselves heard just as lustily. "Come back Tuesday to find out!"

As the people in the crowd turn back to their days, Marco and I are left standing onstage, dumbfounded that Victor has outfoxed us. He enjoys our dismay.

"You thought you pulled a fast one, didn't you? I'm thirty-six, boys. I've lived twice as long as you. And I did not get to be chief seasonal events officer for the Shops at Vision Landing by letting anyone else run my show." He pauses, adopting his version of a gangster glare. "*Never* mess with a millennial."

He's so satisfied right now that it hurts. "Now go do your jobs."

Apparently, I look how I feel, because he adds, "And smile. You don't want to ruin anyone's Christmas."

Christmas Day / Eleventh Day of Elfmas

Christmas morning starts slower than any other day of the year. Dad is a morning person by nature, but even he needs time to sleep off Noche Buena, which involves as much drinking as eating (and both in large amounts). This is a tradition, but not a good idea, and last night he ended up standing on Mari's counter singing "Chandelier," while she swatted at his legs with a kitchen towel, begging him to come down.

As a result of nights like that, it's pretty typical of us to not start presents till almost noon. I was never one of those kids jumping on their parent's bed to wake them early, because presents aren't the focus in our house. Whether Dad realizes it or not, I'm with him in this: Cookie Party is peak Christmas for me, followed by Noche Buena. Presents come third, in part because there's only two of us, so it's not like a ritual that takes very long. My tías always give us gifts, but the pile isn't ever huge. And my dad is a wacky gift giver: sometimes, the presents are just what I dreamed of (AirPods my sophomore year), and some years they leave me scratching my head (case in point: the giant fur-and-suede Yukon trapper hat he gave me last year that I knew cost too much and still would never leave the house in).

This morning, Dad wears the pajamas I got him last year from J. Crew and I'm in a fire-engine-red fleece onesie I like to sleep in on Christmas. "Whose year is it?" he asks, still sounding punished by last night, even though he's been up long enough to bake a tray of apple slippers, their scent perfuming the whole house.

"Mine," I say, donning the felt Santa hat that designates the gift-passer. I hand him the first package, from Ely. He cannot be surprised to find that it's a pair of snowman socks, but he gushes over them as much as if she were here to listen. Holding them up next to his face, he takes a selfie, which is pretty much how we do thank-you cards. I open my present from her, and it's a Zara gift card for a lot more than those socks cost, because she knows me well, and because I am still young enough that grown-ups like to spoil me.

Next are Mari's gifts. For him, a set of dish towels covered in, you guessed it, snowmen. My dad's life is a warning to me to never tell anyone you collect a thing because that is all you will get for eternity. Naturally, he loves the towels and takes a happy selfie to prove it. Because mine is in an envelope, I'm pretty sure it's a gift card too. But it's not for Zara—it's for the campus shop at NYU. I forgot that my tías don't know I might not go back. Dad sees my face and squeezes my shoulder. "You'll get a chance to use it; I know you will."

Forging ahead, I hand him my present. I was going to get him a Dorie Greenspan cookbook, but I couldn't remember which ones he has and it would have been too naked to just ask. So I had to wing it. Within the horribly-wrapped gift box, he finds an old plastic snowman that I pulled off the tree; I have written "I.O.U." on its belly with a Sharpie. He's trying to figure this out, and I explain that I got him a gift card to Snowmanshoppe.com. (I know, I know: if you're not part of the solution, you're part of the problem.) I bring up the site on my phone to distract him from the lack of a physical card. "They have a million kinds, and then you can personalize whatever you pick, so no two snowmen in the world are the same!" I'm selling it, and he's buying it, happily scrolling through his options on-screen. No need to mention that I forgot to order it till, um, 1 a.m. My only defense is that I'm eighteen and my semester sucked.

He hugs me, and I hug him back, relieved that he's so happy. "Open mine," he says eagerly.

His is a modest square wrapped in purple-and-gold paper. I don't comment on the colors, just tear the wrapping and lift the lid off the box inside. Nestled within is one of those View-Master slideshow toys. I hold it up to my eyes, and the first slide is of the actress who plays Catherine of Aragon in *Six*, my favorite musical. The second slide is Lizzo. These must be clues of some kind, but I don't know for what. The third slide is the actress who plays Anne Boleyn from the same show. The fourth is Olivia Rodrigo—

Oh my god. I get it. Dad got me a ticket to the hottest event of the year: *Six: The Arena Show*.

It's a genius concept; in the original musical, the six wives of Henry VIII tell their story as if it's a pop concert. For one night only, it really will be, with Lizzo and Rodrigo, plus Megan Thee Stallion, Rina Sawayama, H.E.R., and Billie Eilish playing the queens. It famously sold out in minutes. It's an *impossible* get.

"How did you do this?" I ask.

"It's easy," he says. "You upload the pictures you want to this place that specializes in personalizing View-Masters—"

"The ticket, Dad! How did you score a ticket?"

He grins slyly. "I signed up for the presale back when Mo first told me about it." (Mo?) "She said she thought of you immediately. It was a little scary, you know me and the internet don't get along, but she stayed on the phone and told me not to close my browser and I didn't, and . . . ta-da!"

Who do I know named Mo? Unless he means *Maureen*. Thinking to ask Ms. Kropp for help was a genius move on his part—she's practically a ticket savant.

"You haven't finished your slideshow!" He nudges me to continue. Lifting the viewer to my eyes again, I click through the remaining wives and their superstar cognates, followed by pics of the arena, from a very, *very* high angle.

He's been counting clicks and knows what I'm seeing. "Your seats aren't great, I know. . . ."

"I'm inside the building—they *rock*." I click to the last

image, the Row NYC hotel, which he knows I love because it has a candy store and a food hall.

"I booked you a room there thinking it would be a fun treat for you and your date." Holy cow, he got *two* tickets? "Nicer than going back to your dorm, eh?" He smiles, pleased with himself. "Make all your friends jealous."

Who has this dad? Seriously, he's working two jobs, and he buys me tickets to the show of the century *and* a hotel room? I throw my arms around him and squeeze him so hard he gasps. I know he's emotional, but I'm the one who starts crying first.

He really believes in my New York life; he sees the City Cam that I've been trying to forget. And he's doing his part to make sure *that* Cam's life has a shot. But there's also no way this was a responsible expense on his part. His love for me has totally junked his practical-dad side. My leaving must have really upended him.

"Thank you," I say, because I can't say the rest. How this amazing gift makes my dilemma even more impossible; his faith tells me to give the city one more shot, yet the cost of the gift tells me I should stay where I am. I kiss him on the cheek, trying to tamp down my tears. "You're the best."

The doorbell version of "Carol of the Bells" breaks up this lovefest. Mari doesn't wait for us to answer, just marches in, shaking snow off her North Face. I hadn't even realized it was snowing, but I can see fat swirling flakes behind her as the door swings shut.

"You forgot this," she says, hefting a near-full grocery bag of

Tupperware containers. She's right: in his call-me-Sia stupor, Dad hadn't snagged any leftovers for Christmas day. She heads into the kitchen, which she knows nearly as well as her own, and reaches into the bag for containers stuffed with black beans and rice, picadillo, tostones (which are never as good the next day), green beans, and flan with guava. My dad looks like he's seen the promised land and hands her Christmas plates from the cupboard.

Mari starts to assemble lunch for us, but I stop her. "Wait! None for me."

She adopts a look of horror. "Since when don't you eat my cooking?"

"I'll eat your cooking," Dad says, encouraging her to keep going.

"I ate it last night. You know I love it. But I'm going to Marco's—"

"Even after that hashtag?" She stares at me in amazement, not plating food till Dad motions for her to continue. "I tell you, he fooled me with those dimples."

"What hashtag?" I brace myself on the island for whatever new torment there is.

"My hands are full," she says. "You have a phone. Use it."

I go to Insta and find #SaveJingle! on my home page. TikTok too. On Twitter, it's the top trending hashtag for Massachusetts.

It's accompanied by a pair of photos: one is of me standing next to Victor during his warm-up, my eyes clearly on the tablet in his hands. I'm wearing my super-insincere "nod and smile" grin, which, in this context, looks smug or even slimy. The second photo is Marco looking sad. Honestly, it's probably just him looking at the floor politely while listening to Victor talk, but it becomes poignant because of the caption: "TFW the vote is rigged." Naturally, the post originated on the timeline of @XmasLvr.

"What the hell?"

"Either he really wants to win, or someone out there doesn't like you very much," Mari says, reading the posts. "#ElfFail . . . #OopsyCheated . . . #OopsyCheatsAgain . . . didn't you say your ingredient was missing too?"

There is a certain comfort in knowing that my paranoia is, at the very least, shared, and may not actually even be paranoia. But that vindication only means someone really is sabotaging me. Who and why must be connected, but who holds that big a grudge? Sure, in school, there were kids I didn't like who returned the favor, but not to a degree that would warrant this campaign. And I have to factor in opportunity: the social media posts would be easy enough to pull off, but the missing ingredient adds a degree of difficulty: someone had to be in the mall at the right time and not be seen as out of place.

Despite what Mari implied, I know @XmasLvr is not Marco. It can't be. Period.

Could it be one of the other elves after all? I don't feel any better allowing that thought either. Maybe Leroy? It seems far-fetched considering he was trying to get us back together at the same time as @XmasLvr was first riling things up. Or his boyfriend? I think of spotting Shay on the day of the bake-off. Did they break up because I'm back?

It's definitely not Victor, who would never do anything that gives 12 Days of Elfmas bad press. Fiona? I mean, I've already discovered she has hidden talents. . . . Is trolling one of them? Maybe Kandy is more of a stalker than I knew. Or even Safety Mom—Wow, I'm reaching.

I'm suddenly just so tired of the whole thing. I need to see Marco, and sooner rather than later. I tell Dad and Mari that I have to go, kiss them each on the cheek, and leave Dad to cure his hangover with pork.

Marco lives in one of those old colonial farmhouses you see in New England, a caterpillar of connected segments: two-story main house connected by a low-rise passage to the barn. It definitely looks weathered by time, but considering it's holding its ground three hundred years after it was built, it's pretty impressive. Marco tells me that when his dad was our age, he supported himself by working for the farmers who owned this land. Years later when he saw that it was for sale, he jumped at the chance, even though Marco's mom, a city girl, initially said she would never live in any house with a barn, much less one attached.

I leave my shoes in the big pile of footwear at the door, and he leads me forward. The house has so much personality, with colorful throws and blankets brightening even the lowest-ceilinged room. A fire is going in an ancient-looking fireplace, their Christmas tree glows with multicolored lights. Star-shaped lanterns hang from the rafters in almost every room.

"Your mom really likes stars, huh?"

Marco sees what I'm looking at. "The parols? That's just a Christmas thing. She *loves* Christmas. The second Labor Day is over, she's on it."

Hmm. She loves Christmas. . . . Dad loves Christmas. . . . She's single. . . . He's single. . . .

"Hungry?" he asks, interrupting my *Parent Trap* fantasy. It isn't like he waits for an answer; he's already nuking a big bowl of fried rice. I wouldn't have said I was hungry a minute ago, but the smell of garlic and oil and something salty makes my stomach growl.

His mom comes in the room and flashes a happy smile to see that he's feeding me, but reminds him that it's family WhatsApp time. She forces Marco to text greetings to assorted titos and titas before she releases us.

We carry our bowls to his room, which is a mash-up of parts of his life I had no clue about. There are Marvel movie posters for *Black Panther* and *Shang-Chi*, but also blow-ups of nature photographs he took, including a sunset in Provincetown that looks like the work of a pro. What I can't get over is a replica painting of Da Vinci's *Last Supper*. "So . . . you're religious?"

"*Mom* is. She says Jesus has to be in every room, and he is— the living room gets his portrait, her room has a crucifix, and the dining room has a painting where it looks like he's lifting off. She let me choose when I was, like, twelve, and I picked this one."

"Why?"

He grins. "Because I think it's funny. Why are they all on one side of the table? Is it like the old version of a selfie but really slow?" I laugh at this. "It keeps her happy, which is all that matters. She's my mom; it's the least I can do to repay her. And it's better than the crucifix, which is super graphic and kind of freaks me out."

I'm so happy sitting here, eating with him (though I cannot figure out the caramelized pink meat in my fried rice). The elf drama seems far away, until he pulls out his phone and brings up the meme, asking, "Any idea who did this?"

"Not a clue!"

"Well, they can give it up. I made my own hashtag!"

He hands me the phone, which shows a close-up of him smiling and not one but three hashtags: #IDontNeedSaving, #NotRigged, and #IHeartOopsy.

A quick look reveals that his reply has been shared hundreds of times already. I hand the phone back. "I mean, do you think it will calm things down?"

"Don't know. But I had to do *something*."

"You didn't have to . . . you *chose* to. You could've just taken the win!"

Instead of answering, Marco eyes my bowl, which I have only half finished. "So . . . not a fan of spam?"

Ah, that solves the pink mystery. "It's good, really good, but between Cookie Party and Noche Buena, I've kinda maxed out my capacity to consume food for a week. And I'm not done—we always get Chinese on Christmas night, so we don't have to cook. My body is actually begging me to stop."

He reaches for the bowl, scooping the remnants into his empty bowl. "Because I am such a good guy, I will save you from further suffering," he jokes.

"You are a good guy," I say, and I'm *not* joking. "And I can't believe I didn't see it right away!"

He sets his once-again-empty bowl on the nightstand and looks at me. "Really? How did I seem?"

I shake my head. "That came out wrong. You always seemed good—no, you seemed *nice*. So nice I was like, 'Ugh.'"

He raises an eyebrow. "Why would you be like 'Ugh' over someone nice?"

It's a fair question. "Maybe because I'm not?" I'm kind of kidding, but not 100 percent.

Marco pulls me close to rest my head on his shoulder. "Talk to me."

"I think since I was little I knew I was different, and different wasn't easy anywhere but home. So I kind of made it my defense to think that everyone else was kind of stupid, or at least not as smart as me. I decided I was cooler than them. More sophisticated. Cheerful people—like really cheerful—I always rolled my eyes at, because *come on. . . .*"

"I've seen you do that!" He looks at me, getting it. "Did you roll your eyes at me?"

"All the time! Those first few days, I was like, 'This guy!'"

Marco nods as he takes this in. "So, in other words . . . you're just an asshole." He says this with a wink, but you know, he's not wrong.

"The last few days make me want not to be, if that helps."

He leans in so that our foreheads are almost touching. "It does, actually." He kisses me, gently, his dark hair falling onto my face. I don't brush it away.

Pulling back after a moment, I tell him about my come-uppance. "When I got to the city, I was surrounded by people who were cooler than their towns too, but suddenly *I* was the one who felt stupid and unsophisticated. I knew they all looked at me like I used to look at the kids in my class."

He sits up, ready to defend me against unseen foes. "What did they do to you?"

I pat his chest. "Nothing—it was more like—"

"What they said?"

"No, not even that . . . I mean . . ."

He frowns. "If they didn't say or do anything, how do you know they even thought of you that way? Maybe it was your inner asshole telling you *they* were assholes when really they were just doing their own thing and not worrying about you at all."

Ouch. "You can be really blunt, you know."

This merits a shrug. "Born this way. When I love someone, I don't censor. My mom says I used to tell her and Dad whatever I thought: if her church dress didn't fit, I told her; if he parked the car badly, I told him; if I thought they were not doing something as well as my friends' parents, I told them that too." He looks wistful. "My dad said I was the only ray of sunshine that came with its own lightning bolt."

I'm stuck on the first part. "When you love someone, huh?"

"Or *like*!" He laughs. "But keep working on it and you may get there." His smile fades. "Did I hurt your feelings, when I said that about it just being in your head?"

"Maybe a tiny bit."

"I think of myself as just telling it like it is. . . ." He rests his head on mine. "But maybe we're all just assholes in our own way."

"Doesn't make you wrong. I have to admit, you have me wondering if I chased *myself* away. Maybe the only one who thought I shouldn't be there was me."

Marco cups my chin in his hands and gives me a searching look. "What do you think now?"

"I think . . ." A feeling comes over me, an awareness that, sitting here on his bed, talking quietly in the half-light of a winter afternoon, I feel truer to myself than I have in many months. And that I'd like to stay this way. "I think New York looks a lot less interesting now that I'm here with you. I could see myself getting used to this."

Marco's eyes sparkle, and I realize he's on the brink of tears.

"If you don't go back," he whispers, "I'll make sure you're glad you stayed."

We sit in the quiet of this vision. I'm picturing a winter of holding each other by the fireplace, arguing over which Netflix show to watch. Spring walks through the nearby orchards as the apple blossoms bloom, even though my allergies will make me pay. Summer days eating fried food on boardwalks after we bake ourselves on the beach. I feel my eyelids growing heavier, and I settle into the beauty of a nap with my boyfriend.

I am dressed as the Emcee in the musical *Cabaret*, which is to say, wearing leather pants and almost nothing else but glitter. Sarah Xu is dragging me by the hand through tunnels and hallways and more tunnels and hallways, and I know that we're at NYU but I can't tell where. "What's going on?" I ask.

"I don't have time for your questions," she snaps. "I have class."

"So what are you doing here?"

Sarah Xu frowns, perplexed. "Getting you to curtain call! I'm the stage manager." I see that she is wearing my elf costume. Was she before? She hurries ahead, so I can't ask.

At last, we arrive at a big red door marked "STAGE," and when she opens it, I can hear the applause of a boisterous crowd. I hesitate.

"Are you coming?" I whisper, which makes her purse her lips.

"I'm not even here! I *told* you I'm in class!"

I know I am in a dream, know the crowd is not real and the cheers aren't either, but I want to step through that door onto the stage so badly. I turn to thank Sarah Xu, but she is gone. The door remains open. The crowd is calling my name. "*Cameron! Cameron! Cameron!*"

It feels. So. Good.

When we wake, Marco's arm has fallen asleep, and he is comically trying to bring it to life. But I feel guilty. One moment I'm saying I'll stay, and literally the next I'm dreaming of leaving. How am I supposed to know what to do?

The room is really dark now, and when I check my phone, it's almost six. Dad has texted to see if I've picked up the Chinese. I tell Marco I need to leave, but we make out a little first, because we can, and it's almost seven before I thank his mom for the Spam fried rice and hop in the car.

Sichuan Gourmet is a family-owned place in the next town that makes all these dishes you don't find at chains like Panda Express. Dry hot chili fish, spicy dan dan, double-cooked bacon—it's all authentic, which makes it feel more special to me, as does knowing that none of my Lindell friends eat there. (Will I ever outgrow being a snob?)

I expect a line—people in the know are pretty passionate about Sichuan Gourmet—but I don't expect this: the person ahead of me is Leroy, who never knew the place existed before he met me.

"Merry Christmas?" I say, pronouncing the question mark as my way of acknowledging that this is awkward.

"Ho, ho, ho," he replies, eyes sliding away from mine. His phone boops and boops, and I'm grateful that he focuses on checking it. The line is not moving very quickly, so we stand there silently while he texts, and I mentally beg the universe to speed up my order.

When his phone settles down for a minute, a half smile plays on his lips. He looks like he wants to say something. But I know he's going to make me start, so I do. "I'm guessing you saw the whole #SaveJingle thing."

"Yeah," he says, eyes flashing. "How's that going for you?"

"What can I say? Some jerk named @XmasLvr hates me."

He doesn't exactly disagree. "Hates you, huh?" His phone boops again, but he keeps his eyes on me this time. "What did you *do* to this guy?"

"*If* it even is a guy. I don't actually know—" I bring up the antagonistic profile on my phone to show him that there's no revealing information, and he raises one eyebrow, like he's amused.

And then I know. It's him after all: Leroy is @XmasLvr.

It rocks me a little. He was doing this at the same time as we were rekindling things? When we kissed by the pond, he'd already created #ElfFail! "Oh my god!"

He looks kind of satisfied at the shock on my face, but the line shuffles ahead and he turns away for a moment.

When the line is immobile again, I make him face me. "Why? I know we broke up—"

"You broke up with me."

"And you *said* you understood—that long distance didn't make any sense."

His eyes widen. "What did you expect me to say? I wasn't about to *beg* you! Don't you get it?" He stops as if stunned by my idiocy. "You broke my heart!"

His words betray no sarcasm, no hint of exaggeration. He means it. I honestly had never believed this could be true. "But . . . but . . ."

"But what? You were my first boyfriend, you know." His eyes burrow into mine, trying to imagine how I could be so clueless.

"I didn't think you were that into me, I guess. And you dated the twink from summer camp, like, seconds later."

He palms his forehead. "That's what you call a rebound. I liked dating. I liked knowing you were there and then suddenly you were all 'I need to move on' and I was alone. At first, Shay just filled the place I wanted you to be."

I hear him, but how is he making me the bad guy? It's not like I doomed him to a life of celibacy. He didn't have to break up with Shay when I came back. "Okay, but you weren't alone. And you don't have to be now. Not for me."

"Who says I am?" Leroy eyes me coolly.

"Wait—did you not break up?"

The line inches forward again, and Leroy is next. But he's

focused on this conversation. "Why would I? I'm sure you scorn him like you do everything else in this town, but he's a decent guy. I'm starting to be happy again."

"So the pond . . . the kiss . . . Why *do* all this?"

He thinks about this. "I wanted to take you down a peg. Let you know what it feels like to *not* get what you want." It's quiet. And then a rueful sigh. "Guess that didn't work."

"Trust me," I say, "the universe covered that for you."

His expression softens. "What do you mean?"

"I blew it at school and can only afford to go back if I win this."

"Huh," he murmurs. "That's news."

"Leroy? LEROY?" Mrs. Li calls his name and he steps forward to pay.

When he's finished, he turns to me, almost shy, and at the same time, we both say, "I'm sorry." And we laugh.

"Think you have any chance tomorrow?" he asks.

"Hard to say. But it's not too late for you to vote for me, unless you really do want all the money to go to my boyfriend." I swear the word just slips out, and it's too late to take it back.

"Boyfriend?" He groans and then mutters, "Is there any way you can both lose?"

"Probably," I joke. "And at this point it wouldn't even surprise me."

Jazz and I video chat after I've crawled into bed. My room is dark, the glow of my phone a campfire to warm myself by. She says Annika is asleep and snoring, which Jazz is still not used to, so she is calling me from the big club chair in the living room, her favorite place in the house. I can see the tree lights twinkling behind her. It's just us now, in our quiet homes, carrying on a conversation that's been rolling along for years but may be winding down, even if we can't admit it.

"I'm thinking about spending the summer in Rødøya," she tells me, and I know from the set of her voice that this is not a thought but a plan.

"That sounds Norwegian," I say, trying to stifle my disappointment. Whether or not I spend the spring at NYU, I already had plans for Jazz and me this summer. I've already started looking at cabins on lakes for a weekend, and I'd printed out the whole lineup at the concert pavilion on Boston Harbor that we like.

"Yeah, Rødøya's the island Annika's from. . . ." As she extolls the isle's virtues (mountains, beaches, and, I guess, cod), I process the loss of the day trips that will never materialize now. I know I need to be happy for her. And that she needs to hear it.

"I'm glad you found someone," I finally say.

"Awww. You too."

We don't say anything else for a minute or two. I think we both understand that our lives are rolling ahead on paths that will converge less and less. It's almost unimaginable to think of a world in which I'm not close to Jazz, not a big part of her life, but isn't that what this first semester has been practice for? Isn't that what this time in life is all about?

I stare at her beautiful face on the glowing screen. It's too soon, way too soon, to say "Goodbye, old friend." Too soon to close the door on this time in our lives for good. But we're on the threshold.

Twelfth—and Last—Day of Elfmas

I've been enjoying my shower so long that the bathroom looks like a rain forest: billowing foggy clouds fill it from floor to ceiling. As long as I stay in here, I don't have to face the music.

Before I got out of bed, I made a decision: I'll let the universe, in the form of my fellow citizens of the Pioneer Valley, determine whether I go back to NYU. If I win the money, replacing the lost scholarship, I need to see things through and return to school. If I'm lucky, the school will let me switch majors and I can see if Musical Theatre is a better fit. But, if I lose, I won't force more of a financial burden on my dad; I'll stay here and be grateful for the time I have with Marco.

"Are you ever getting out?" Dad raps at the door, something he almost never does, even though we only have one bathroom and I'm a lingerer. "You're not the only one who needs to shower!"

"Coming," I call, drying off and wrapping myself in a towel. I wipe a spot on the fogged-up mirror to see myself. I look into my own eyes and wonder what Marco sees in them. Thinking of him makes me smile, and I use my fingertip on a still-foggy section of the mirror to write his name inside a heart, with an arrow. God, he's upended me.

When I open the door, Dad is standing there, impatient, clothes in hand. Instead of a holiday sweater (a look he typically milks till at least New Year's), he has a sleek checked shirt and a complimentary crew-neck sweater, both of which I bought him. This is as dressed-up as Dad ever gets.

"Are you making us go to Mass or something?"

"No, today we all just worship you." He chuckles. "No chance I'm missing the finale. You knew I'd come, right?"

"Good," I say. "I'll need you."

"Did you just say that out loud?" He pretends to faint.

I roll my eyes. "Just shower. You kinda stink."

Dad honks, and I hurry outside.

A box sits on the front steps, and it makes my heart smile to see it. Jazz and I have been doing our Boxing Day tradition even longer than our Wright Brothers thing. When we were in elementary school, we thought it had something to do with boxers, not boxes, but then our teacher told us it was a day the poor were given presents by those with money. The day after Christmas that year, Jazz showed up at my house with a satiny hatbox full of stocking stuffers she had decided to pass on to me.

I still remember my shock: Jazz thought I was poor.

I had stood there, jaw on the floor. Dad didn't have a second job then, so things were a little tight, but I had no idea she, in all her middle-class glory, thought of me like that. I was so mad that I slammed the door in her face. Jazz being Jazz, she pestered me until I let her inside and we talked it out. What did we know about real poverty or real wealth? We were nine-year-olds in farm country. We agreed that if she kept half and I kept half, then we were equal, instead of her being somehow above me. I didn't admit it, but I was really psyched to get a light-up toothbrush in the deal, and I kept the hatbox, which I thought was cool.

The next year, I left the hatbox on her doorstep. It was empty except for a note: "Nothing for you, rich girl! Happy Boxing Day." And because we're us, a tradition was born: we pass the box back and forth year after year. Sometimes there are presents inside, sometimes just a funny note. One year, it was full of printouts of texts revealing my mortifying crush on an exchange student from Thailand who was painfully straight.

When I lift the top today, I find inside a Polaroid of me and Jazz at age nine, dressed in costume as the lead characters of our favorite show, *Shake It Up*: her sequined to death as Rocky and me in a fedora and red wig as CeCe. I haven't seen this picture in years, but knowing it's from the same year as we started Boxing Day feels both like a way to close the loop and a reminder that we're timeless. I *love* Jazz.

Dad honks again. I tuck the photo into my pocket, leave the hatbox in my house, and head for the car. My chariot, like my future, awaits.

When Dad drops me off by the main mall entrance, he tells me he loves me. "Look for us. We'll be cheering from the galleries on the J. Crew side!" I know Mari and Ely will probably make the cousins show up, so if I lose, I'll at least have my own fan club to cry foul.

I stop by the food court to fortify myself with the largest iced coffee possible before facing the music. I'm expecting Victor to be pretty snarky today, seeing as I haven't seen him since his cat-ate-the-canary power move on Christmas Eve.

But when I walk into the command center, he greets me with his tablet, acting like we're besties. "You two are geniuses. This whole #SaveJingle/#IHeartOopsy drama is selling big. More votes, more visits, more impressions than the rest of the week combined. And the bosses notice this sort of thing." He lets out a dreamy sigh. "Forget seasonal events—this whole mall is gonna be mine."

He thinks we set this up? Fine, let him. If it keeps him happy, that's one less thing to worry about.

Fiona comes in, ready for one last round as Mrs. Claus, and *hugs* me. It is a massive understatement to say I never imagined being on hugging terms with her, and I'm thrown. Do I hug back? I end up patting her awkwardly, like I'm soothing a giant Irish baby.

When she pulls away, she tells me that the performance went viral on YouTube and she's gotten a bunch of licensing requests for the song. Most important, "I heard from someone who works with Pentatonix. *Pentatonix!*" She's breathless with excitement. "Next year," she says, "*someone else* can play Mrs. Claus!"

I congratulate her, ducking just out of hug range in case she wants a refill, while looking for Marco. There's only fifteen minutes before we go on, and we still have some secret business to take care of before we do. Where is he?

I see motion in one of the changing booths and make a beeline for it. "Marco?"

Leroy pulls back the curtain. "Sorry to disappoint you."

"Oh, hi . . ."

He looks away briefly, biting his lip, and then looks back. "Good luck today."

I have the distinct feeling that he wants to say more, but he doesn't—maybe he can't. Or maybe he said more than he wanted to last night. He wasn't raised by my dad; communicating his feelings might be as foreign to him as, like, home repairs are to me. It feels like it's on me to break the spell. "Did I get your vote?"

"Sure," he says in his one-syllable deadpan, but his eyes won't meet mine.

Now it's only ten minutes till showtime. You can hear the crowd from inside the command center and still no Marco. I don't care if it makes me late: I'm going to look for him soon. Where exactly, I don't know. We're not at the Find My Friends app stage of our relationship yet, so I can't even ping his location.

When he finally rushes in—already dressed, thank god—I feel about a thousand times better. "Where were you?"

"Picking this up!" He waves a Santaland photo sleeve and flashes that smile I love so much.

Yesterday, while snuggled together on his bed, he told me how he'd kept an eye all week on Safety Mom, whose real name is Maya, which (Marco being typically Marco) he had learned days ago. He could tell how bad she felt about coming day after day without buying anything. It was me trying to be *better* than typical me who had the idea of surprising her and the kids with a two-elf visit today and a present.

As we head for the door to find them, Victor's eyes widen. "Where do you think you're going?"

"We'll be right back!" I promise, pretty much pushing Marco out of the room.

"If you are not here in eight minutes—" We let the door close on his threat and don't wait to hear the rest. What can he really do? We're the stars of the show!

We find the family by the reindeer, Kumar and Anjali trying to replicate the deer's movements. Maya is staring at her phone, brow creased with worry.

"Maya?" Marco calls, and she looks up, face softening on sight. I wonder just how many people in the world he has had that effect on.

He passes the folder to me, I guess since it was my idea. She looks puzzled, even more so, when I say, "We found this. You, uh, left it behind by accident."

She reaches for the folder, and I can see a slow dawning on her face even before she opens it to see the photos. We'd talked the photographer into looking through his trash files to find the best ones of Anjali and Kumar. Marco and I chipped in to print up a full set to give her, assuming she and the kids came back today.

Her lips part, but she says nothing at first, perhaps worried that there has been some mistake. Marco gives her a wink and says, "Winning the free photo giveaway but then forgetting them at the booth would have been a shame, right?"

The kids are practically climbing her to see the pictures as she answers, "You have no idea . . ." She kneels down so they can see better, and mouths, "Thank you," eyes wet, and that seems like our cue to go.

Outside the door to the command center, Marco stops me. "Who's the nice one now?"

"That was pretty great, right?"

"The question is, are you gonna roll your eyes at *yourself*?"

"All day long," I say, feeling impossibly lucky to have met him. And I kiss him, so glad to know that this is real. It's a great kiss that I hate to end. Seriously, I'd love to attempt a Guinness World Record for kissing with him, but I know people are waiting for us, and I reluctantly pull away.

Good thing I do, as Victor flings the door open, clapping. "Can you not read a clock? You're on!"

Working our way through the throng, I bump into Kandy leading a phalanx of girls and boys wearing my face on T-shirts. They've taken Marco's IHeartOopsy hashtag and made it their own. They swarm me for a group shot, Victor hissing, "Not now! Not now!" as if Kandy has ever been dissuaded from anything.

When Kandy clicks the last photo, I have to ask. "Why me? Why all this?"

Her smile is immense. "What can I say? I'm an enthusiast. If you think this is a lot, you should see what I do for BLACK-PINK."

Marco seems similarly ensconced in a throng, and Victor is losing his mind. He physically extricates both of us and steers us toward the stage, muttering about how next year he's hiring professionals.

The crowd is vast and all keyed up; I try to just soak the moment in.

A mere two weeks ago, I thought I had actually failed my classes. I thought Sarah Xu saw me as a talentless bumpkin. I didn't know that the Shops at Vision Landing were open or that I would work there in any capacity, much less as an elf. More than that, I didn't have a boyfriend I adore. But here I am. Life is a trip: you just can't see what you can't see until it materializes in front of your eyes.

Call me shallow, but I'm loving this. For a moment, I pretend it's a Broadway audience before me, full of people who came to the show because I am in it. There's a boy at the stage door waiting for me to sign the Playbill he will hang up in his room. And a critic is already running for their train so they can get home and write the rave review I deserve.

I'm going to win. I know this in my body all at once, and it's a jolt. I'm going to win and go back to NYU and try again. City Cam isn't gone yet; he's just getting started.

Scanning the crowd, I see Miranda and Raven with all their younger siblings and their parents too. I can't imagine the Book of Mormon encourages cheering on homosexuals, but what do I know? *Nothing*. I know nothing. They're definitely scoring in the raising-decent-humans department, so when they look my way, I make sure to wave and mouth, "Thank you for coming."

Larry and his wife are right up front, chatting with Marco's mom like old friends. She's having a good time as far as I can tell, but I wish I'd arranged for her to meet Dad here. I make a promise to myself that I will set them up. You never know: after a little your-elf-likes-my-elf bonding, maybe they'll get some ideas of their own.

I finally see Jazz and Annika, up in the second gallery with my tías, assorted younger cousins, Dad, and Ms. Kropp. I guess she's a regular now.

Victor takes the mic. "I don't know about you, but I think this has been the BEST CHRISTMAS EVER!" The crowd applauds the claim—well, not the whole crowd. Because my Dad isn't looking at Victor: he's giving Ms. Kropp a kiss.

Thank god I don't have to sing today, because I am speechless. Mr. "Boo Hoo, You Didn't Confide in Me" is seeing my favorite teacher? Why couldn't he have done this when I was home to appreciate it? And why not tell me?

Ignoring whatever Victor is droning on about, I tug Marco's hand and whisper, "My dad is with Ms. Kropp!" I point at the sneaky liars accusingly.

"Yeah. I know. She was at the party."

Wait—he's known since Saturday? Does everyone know but me? How clueless am I? Suddenly I remember the Snowmamas.

Victor's voice pierces my fog. "It all comes down to this. . . ."

Someone in the galleries starts a drumroll, and others pick it up, adding tension to a moment that didn't need more.

Marco takes my hand in his. "I hope you win," he says softly.

"I hope *you* do," I say back.

And then he grins. "I might be lying."

I just laugh. "I might be too."

"The winner of Top Elf is . . ."

Universe, listen, can you slow down time? Hold the answer at bay as long as you can. Let me enjoy not knowing how the money will divide us into before and after. Please—

"JINGLE!"

The cheering and applause are deafening. My heart falls, as NYU recedes like a fading memory. Broadway is gone, taking with it the boy holding a Playbill and the critic who will never know my name. The universe has other plans for me.

But since I *am* a nice guy, one who has a great boyfriend, and this is *his* moment, I let out a whoop and throw my arms around him. His eyes are full of tears, and I know how much he needs this, no matter what he said. I have all the time in the world to feel blue for me; right now, I'm just so happy for him. When Fiona hands him a giant five-thousand-dollar check with his name on it, camera flashes in the crowd sparkle like waves in sunlight.

"Calm down, calm down!" Victor is admonishing. "There's more!"

Larry and his wife are making their way up the stairs of the bandstand. Whatever is about to happen, he's enjoying it. Larry takes the mic. "What Victor didn't say is that it was a dead heat. Just about a tie," he says. The crowd starts murmuring. Where is this going?

"The rules say the five thousand dollars can't be split. But you can always get around a rule somehow, right, Oopsy?" He winks at me before going on. "Now, I know you all saw me as an elf, but I'm more of a Santa guy."

He signals someone in the back of the crowd. Kandy and Leroy thread their way forward, carrying *another* giant check, its face covered, and the audience starts to applaud.

No way.

"We saw both these boys sing. We heard them. You all know it wasn't a one-person show, so it makes no sense to make it a one-person prize. Fortunately, it just so happens that I married the chief operating officer of the EFE!"

His wife leans into the mic. "That's Equity for Elves, if

you don't know." When this earns laughs, she pretends to take offense. "This is serious business!" It's a great bit: she fake glares at whoever laughed, and Larry wags a stern finger. They're clearly enjoying themselves.

I'm holding my breath. Just how big is this check?

Leroy and Kandy reach the stage and hand the check to Larry's wife, who passes the mic back to her husband. "No rule says there can't be *two* prizes. So, without further ado . . ." With his free hand, Larry flips the sheet to reveal my name and the full five thousand dollars.

Marco is so happy he can't help himself. He grabs me, lifting me off my feet, and gives me a kiss for the ages. And then we face the crowd, richer than we were just moments ago, and raise our clasped hands in the air. Victorious.

Back in the command center, we each get real checks and thank our benefactors. "Are you sure you can afford this?" I ask Larry. "I mean, you're a retiree. . . ."

He winces. "That is a terrible word. Ask Michelle here, I don't allow it in my presence." She nods, chuckling. "'Retiree' is a condition; I'm just *retired*—which is nothing more than a schedule adjustment."

"You think *he's* paying for this?" Michelle laughs. "Did he not mention that I'm a banker?" Larry looks sheepish. She does a pretty good imitation of him: "'I was a *general*, you know. . . . Oh, and my wife runs Pioneer Savings or something. . . .'" And she gives him a playful poke in the arm.

Marco thanks Victor for everything, and Victor looks smug. "I knew you'd win. I called it from the start." He shoots me a sideways look. "*You* . . . you just be glad I let these two help you out."

"Like you could've stopped us," Larry says. "What is it you keep saying? 'It's all about impressions'? Well, I think that made a major impression."

Miranda and Raven burst into the room, Miranda throwing her arms around both Marco and me at once. "That was the best!" she exclaims, and then hugs Larry too.

Fiona asks for a group shot of just the elves, and we all put our arms around each other, except for Raven. "Still not a hugger," they say, "but my sister's right. This really was the best."

On the count of three, we flash our brightest smiles for the camera and the camera flashes back.

And just like that, the 12 Days of Elfmas are over.

First Day of the Rest of Our Lives

The snowshoes are Marco's idea. The day is perfectly clear, the sky so blue it can't be real, and the sun is making everything shine. Last night, when we finally stopped making out for a few minutes, he said he'd found his parents' old snowshoes in the attic and wanted to try them out. I agreed, though I have never done any sport involving boots and poles, because at this point, I think I'd agree to anything that allows me to spend more time with Marco. (Unless he wanted to watch a Patriots game. I mean, I have limits.)

I wouldn't say I'm a natural at this. I feel awkard, like a baby duck with enormous feet, but the state park he brought me to more than makes up for it with beauty. I'm wearing my North Face parka, because I'm focused on the experience itself, not the pictures we might take. We follow a snowy trail through old-growth evergreens, rarely encountering anyone else. Sometimes, when we pause to let me collect my breath, we just listen to the not-quite-silence: wind moving through the bows, morning birdsong, the rat-a-tat drumming of a wood-pecker at work.

He tells me stories about his childhood as we wind our way uphill to a lookout. When he was seven or eight, he had a crush on a neighbor boy and picked the kid a bouquet's worth of wild roses in a field. This is how he discovered two things: your average second-grade boy is not prepared to have a smitten classmate show up on his doorstep with flowers, *and* that the roses were not wild at all but carefully tended by the boy's mother, who was growing them for the state fair.

But with every adorable story, I find it harder to listen. I need to talk to him about us. About me. *Leaving.*

It's hard to imagine giving up Marco so soon after we found each other. There's something about him that makes me feel different than I ever have. Electricity. Joy. Playfulness. *Aspiration.* When I'm with him, I not only want to be my best self but can imagine it. Like I will become kinder, more thoughtful, simply by osmosis. Except you need to be around someone for osmosis to work, and I won't be much longer. I have to tell him this.

A spray of icy crystals hits me. Marco shakes the limb of a snow-laden tree so that it showers me. "What was that?"

"You were zoning out. I just saved you from a coma."

"My hero?" I say, pronouncing the question mark. He just laughs and heads farther up the hill, assuring me that it's not far now.

He's right. In a matter of minutes, the trees give way to a clearing, and I hear him softly murmur, "Look!" I join him, and we just stand there, side by side, soaking in the view. The valley fans out below us, snow-covered fields laced with old stone walls, punctuated with stands of maples now bare, and the occasional abandoned hay bale. Beyond, the evergreens start up again, wintry sentinels marching to the horizon.

"It's gorgeous." I speak in a whisper, feeling like I need to honor the serenity.

"I am?" he says, eyes twinkling.

"*It* is. The valley!"

"So I'm *not*, then?"

I punch his arm. "Both can be true. It is . . . *and* you are. . . ." Here it comes again, the sinking feeling that I have something amazing and I'm going to leave it behind. I lean against him, eyes on the valley, heart in my throat.

The woodpecker taps out secret messages. Faintly, I hear cars miles away. Someone in the woods is whistling.

Marco says it for me. "You're going back, right?"

I nod, eyes full of tears.

"Good." He gulps. "Good." He drops his walking pole and pulls me closer.

"Glad to get rid of me, huh?" I use a mitten to wipe my eyes.

"*So* glad! I've always said my first relationship should only last a few weeks. This just sticks to the plan. Next guy gets a whole month."

I pull away from him. "*Next* guy?"

"Oh yeah, I have a full schedule lined up," he jokes wryly. "Bet I look less nice to you now."

"No chance," I say, and I mean it. "You're kinda perfect."

His cool cracks a little, and he sweeps me into an embrace. "I'm a jerk," he says. "I know I said I wanted you to win, but I also wanted you to lose. So you'd *have* to stay. I'm a shitty human."

"Are you kidding? I want to be with you so much, and still I held my breath yesterday hoping Victor would say *my* name. When he said yours instead, the disappointment hit me like a gut punch. We're *not* shitty, either of us." I try to lighten the mood. "We're winners!"

"So why does it feel—"

"Like we're losing something?" It's a question I've been asking all day. He starts to cry.

"Maybe," I say, a little shyly, afraid this might be too much, "because it's special?" He blinks away his tears and looks me in the eye. "I mean, thirteen days ago I wouldn't have imagined this at all, much less how good it is, but . . . it's not just something new. It's *different*. I haven't felt this way about anyone before."

"I feel it too," he says, his eyes wet. "And I want to enjoy it, but I keep thinking about . . ."

January. School. The miles between us. They loom before us without him finishing the thought.

"I know," I whisper, and I kiss him again. "I know."

He sighs. "So what do we do now?"

"You're the one with the plan. Check the instruction manual

to see how you're supposed to handle your first long-distance relationship."

"You mean it?" he says.

"Why wouldn't I?"

"You think it can work?"

I shrug. "Well, I'm living proof the buses run both directions. I'll only be four hours away from my boyfriend at any moment, and he'll only be four away from me."

He considers this. "What if you forget me once you're back in the city?"

"Will *you* forget *me*?"

"That would be literally impossible!"

"Then that's your answer."

I lean in for a kiss. We hold each other for a long moment, lips speaking a language unique to us. When the kiss ends, we stand there, forehead to forehead, warm despite the cold. "You're stuck with me," I say.

"We'll see about that!" he jokes, backing up.

"Don't even try it!" I try grabbing his parka to pull him close, but he snowshoes out of my grasp. We're both laughing. "Come back here!"

For someone walking on the equivalent of tennis racquets, he dodges me easily. "I forgot to warn you that I won Top Snowshoer last year, and there was no pity prize for second place then."

"Oh yeah? Well, *I* didn't completely fail stage combat!" I

lunge for him but trip over my own feet, and before we can process what's happening, we are tumbling downhill in a jumble of snowshoes and poles.

We laugh so hard, lying in the drifts, that I can't even see for a moment. When I catch my breath and open my eyes, he pulls me toward him. I snuggle close, my head on his chest, and settle in as our breathing syncs up. There are no clouds above to decipher, just open sky as limitless as the future.

Marco starts to sit up, but I use my body to hold him in place.

"Stay there." I sigh.

I curl toward him, feeling as safe as I can ever remember feeling, and press my fingers to his lips. "I'm right where I need to be."

And for the first time in months, I know for sure it's true.

Acknowledgments

Some seasons can feel a little dark. Winter 2021–2022 was rough for me, a time of loss and a deep need to reboot. When Stephanie Guerdan from HarperTeen reached out to my agent to see if I might be interested in writing a Christmas rom-com for gay teens, it was like the universe dropping a gift into my lap at the exact right moment. It was not just the right time but the right person: I am a Christmas whore of the highest order.

Seriously, you cannot imagine how Christmassy I am. One of my earliest memories is lying on the floor of my grandmother's house playing with glittery tinsel. (Try this at home kids: hold a strand over a hot-air vent and you can make it fly!) I collected Christmas Around the World books and played Scrooge in my high school musical. Like Cam's dad, I've been holding a cookie party for decades—even during COVID, where my long-suffering friends had to stand outside in the snow to get their treats. (Naturally, my personal Ho-Ho-Homo holiday playlist is ten hours long.)

It's a good thing I love Christmas, because the offer for this book came while I was teaching seven college classes—pro tip, *never do that*—and I was only able to finish by holing up out of town, away from my daughter, my dog, and my friends the moment the semester ended. Thanks, Lily, for being a good sport about my unexpected away time.

Thanks too to Stephanie Guerdan, who made the entire process a delight, and my agent, Annie Bomke, for sealing the deal. I'm lucky and grateful to have such good people to work with.

I hope this book makes you laugh, sigh, and swoon a little, and that you come away smiling. *Finding My Elf* was the kick start to what turned out to be a pretty wonderful year for me. If there's anything to learn from me and from Cam, it's this: stay open to joy—it could be just around the corner.